To Mr. Sherwood.
MERRY CHRISTMAS!

Thank you for teaching the Challenge Program and taking us on the exciting trips!

↑ a salmon.

Dec 12/06

The New World Triology

Swords and Snakes

by

That Kid

Bloomington, IN   Milton Keynes, UK

authorHOUSE®

AuthorHouse™
1663 Liberty Drive, Suite 200
Bloomington, IN 47403
www.authorhouse.com
Phone: 1-800-839-8640

AuthorHouse™ UK Ltd.
500 Avebury Boulevard
Central Milton Keynes, MK9 2BE
www.authorhouse.co.uk
Phone: 08001974150

First published by AuthorHouse 11/10/2006

ISBN: 1-4259-6052-9 (sc)

Printed in the United States of America
Bloomington, Indiana

This book is printed on acid-free paper.

I dedicate this novel to my mother Wendy who motivated my writing career, Peggy Trendell-Jensen, my fantastic editor and writing teacher, and Barbara Yearsley, an author and elder who told me to be myself in writing, make your writing original. I also have to thank my two grade four teachers Ms. Livingston and Mrs. Nicolls for teaching me social studies, math, science and Language Arts. All that knowledge helped in the production of this novel. And, I need to be grateful to my grade five teachers Mrs. Penner and Ms. Butler who taught me so much vocabulary and gave me challenges that improved my understanding of all subjects. Thanks to my very pro illustrator Jennifer, I have three beautiful drawings in this novel. Thank you all my friends who gave me support in bad times and shared my happiness in my good times. I could have never have completed this novel without all of you!

That Kid

Ch 1 The Portal

The Earth was at war with invading aliens!! Mechs and tanks are stomping and rolling through the futuristic cities. But still, normal life was intact, just with guards patrolling the streets and some run-down buildings. The weather was mildly chilly, since it was late winter, except the occasional blast of heat from the explosions. If you were wondering what a mech was, it is a giant fighting robot with serious weaponry. Four ordinary kids, two girls, two boys. They were all friends and were entering the subway station to take the Hetoreum City subway to their school.

"Max!" yelled Diamond. "Hurry, we need to be at the station by 12:50pm! You're 11 years old! Run faster!"

Max had accidentally slept in because his alarm clock just broke down in the middle of the night!!! Now they were running late.

"Why don't you run faster, you're lagging behind, and you're ten!" replied Max

"Well I need to be beside you because I need to yell at you!"

"I wish I took my speed rockets." Grumbled Max.

"Well too bad!" yelled Diamond.

But sadly they arrived at the subway at 1:00pm and that time was the busiest time of all. It's because many people went to work at 1:00pm because the wars started from 6:00am to 12:00 am. Now they could have made their train but Diamond spent 10 minutes yelling at Max for sleeping in and not changing quickly enough! Suddenly a horn blew and the hologram announcer said

"All passengers of the Hectoreum City Express please go to… but the children never heard what the announcer had said because the marching of the armed soldiers that checked everyone's passport came by. After their passport was checked they had to rely on Sarah's nine year old memory cause' she once saw the station number. It was their first time on plasma powered subway to their school because their parents had to run special errands and the kids didn't know anything about riding this particular train. It took away another 8 precious minutes. By then all trains would leave the station so they dashed to the #67 port. Alas, Max had made them too late because the train just commenced moving and laser stun gate just closed. K.T leaped a desperate leap to reach the subway. He was too short to reach it and got electrified in the gate.

"Yeowwwwwwwwwwwwwwwww!!!!!!!!" he cried.

"Oh perfect, thanks a lot for getting us late, Max, now we are really late for school!!!!" screamed Diamond.

"Hey, don't blame it on Max; it's just going to be a normal day at school, what could go haywire?" said Sarah defensively.

K.T began to weep. He was an eight year old kid so he would cry a lot. He was very emotional.

"We are going to miss school and we are having a Year-end exam. It is most important and if we delay it or miss it, there will be no second attempt to do it again!! We'll miss it and have straight F's on our report cards and be expelled from school!!" he wailed.

"Don't worry," said Sarah soothingly, patting K.T's back, "Another subway will arrive in time and we have our exam at the end of the school day."

"I hope." said Diamond still fuming.

5 hours later… at school…

"Alright your hour to do your year-end exam has disintegrated! Please pass your papers to your mechanical test launchers and program them to launch it into this box" the teacher said

"Oh, Diamond, K.T, Sarah, and Max are extremely late and I despise those kids and I can't wait to expel them!!! Muahahahahahah!!!" added the teacher darkly but forgot she was speaking out loud.

"Um, hello, were right in front of you, we can hear every word you're saying." Said the class.

"Uh, … you did not hear anything…" said the teacher as she waved her hands in a hypnotizing motion. Suddenly the class had no memory of what the teacher had said out loud.

At the subway station…

As the kids were trapped in the subway station.

"Man, school has ended and we're stuck here like a mouse in a mousetrap!!!" wailed K.T

"Look, let's just keep our minds off things by playing our Gameboys from home. I've got new games like Cloud Hunters and the Silencers." Said Diamond, her anger gone and she was cheering up.

4 hours later…

"This is getting boring!!!" yelled Max into the silent room.

They had been locked in at the subway station and couldn't get home because the titanium doors slam shut promptly at 9:00pm and they were too occupied in eating their lunches (dinner) and it was too late to pack up their nourishment and dash to the door. So they had to spend the night here. Since there was no beds they were forced to sleep on the floor or the benches. No pillows were available so used their knapsacks for pillows and it was most unpleasantly uncomfortable. Also they looked like beggars on the street.

14 hours later…

"Ow! Hey! Who kicked my head?!!!" Sarah shouted, massaging her throbbing skull.

All of them awoke with a start and to see that the hologram clock was at the time of 1:00 and the station was bustling with people.

"Ack!!! We've occupied the station for 24 hours!!!" cried Max.

"Second subway for Hectoreum City, all aboard!!" the announcer said.

The kids rushed to the open doors only to observe that the car and every other car were deserted. As the train left, the kids heard a guy whisper sorrowfully to his partner.

"Poor kids, that particular train is supposed to be cursed for all eternity." He said.

"Yeah, that train is supposed to make everyone that goes on it disappear." Said the other guy.

Ch 2 Planet
Mythical Peace

The train ride was very enjoyable without a single hint of a curse. Very comfy chairs and footrests and excellent view. But all of that no-curse stuff ended abruptly when the subway had picked up speed and stations whipped by. All of a sudden the kids' hair was whipping back furiously as though trying to rip and tear itself out of the flesh of the head. There was a smashing noise as the train burst out of the stone, iron, and plasma walls with such force that Max, Sarah, K.T, and Diamond were thrown to the back of the subway and collided painfully with a wall. Out the window the blue and white streaks of cloud and sky quickly zipped away and endless black filled with streaks of white darts as stars flew past. Diamond worried that they might not be able to inhale and exhale properly, but they breathed just fine. A warp of time and distance opened and the train flew right through it. That warp was called the Hyperspace. It allowed the user to cross through half of the universe in a margin of one second! Stars and even planets whizzed past and very soon the subway made a landing on an undiscovered planet of lush forests and towering mountains. Finally the subway came to a stop on the grassy fields.

Suddenly something appeared that didn't show in Earth. The separating parts of the subway snapped together and a hatch swung up from the front of the train and a dragon head emerged. Twin claws appeared magically on the side. The serpentine dragon reared its head, shifted from its subway guise into deep green scales and muttered to himself.

"After my delivery of the fine young children who bring peace to this planet I will have a great slumber for a thousand years." And it took off.

"Hey you stupid dragon! How can we get off this planet?" yelled Sarah angrily.

"A four person star ship lies at the top of the Makari Volcano beyond the Mountains of Shadow and Fire, or otherwise known as The Nightmare Mountains. A hyperspace is also there."

It said as it flew toward the East. Now the four children they observed their surroundings. It was a paradise, wide grassy fields, pure and non-polluted lakes, clean and fresh air, even under the ground, (when

Max dug for fun) a substance called The Blue Nectar provided (if cars and buildings were built) non-pollutant oil and also you pour one drop of the substance onto garbage and waste and barren and polluted land, the land will heal and the garbage will disappear into thin air so it won't pollute lakes. The air was so fresh that anyone who inhaled it would feel peaceful so there would be no fighting or wars. It was a perfect place compared to Earth to live but all of Earth's population didn't know about this secret planet.

Ch 3 The power Armors

So K.T, Sarah, Max and Diamond journeyed West to the opposite direction the dragon flew in. Along the path they encountered many strange creatures, like the macow which was a macaw but had horns and udders which produced foul-tasting milk only their chicks loved and it could fly up to an altitude 100,000 feet. The liontelope was an antelope but had wickedly sharp fangs, a magenta colored lion mane and paws instead of hooves. A chameleon with bee stingers filled with poisonous venom lined along its sides and had a yellow spotted frill a buzzaleon was. The largest creature they met was an elephanboonba, it was an elephant but its face was red with a blue stripe running down its face and onto its belly. Also it had no tail but it had the distinctive red butt of a baboon. It was covered with white and black fur.

"Gawka, gawka!!!" high above the air a young macow squawked, happy to be flying for the first time. Suddenly a ball of fire came blasting out of nowhere! It struck the young macow on the wing and it started to fall. K.T, who had a love for birds, started chasing it.

"Don't waste your energy!!" cried Diamond.

K.T accidentally fell into this chasm which was two meters deep. The others caught up and descended into the chasm.

K.T's sharp eyes spotted a cylinder of energy with a hovering night-black, split-up and lightning bolt decorated armor with air vents on the chest and arm armor inside the cylinder. K.T also spotted an ipod like thing with a slit on the left side attached to the chest armor. Diamond, Sarah, and Max all tried to enter the cylinder but were bounced back. K.T tried to enter and he penetrated the cylinder as if it weren't there. He took the ipod like thing and it started to talk from a speaker.

"Greetings, one of the four young Galactic Protectors, I am the Speed access device. You may call me Speedo." K.T pressed a button on Speedo and it suddenly shot a narrow beam of red light from the screen onto K.T's left hand. His left hand had three rings of the same energy that made up the cylinder circling his hand. Two rings encircled diagonally while one circled horizontally.

"No!!!" cried Sarah as she raised he head and saw the macow falling one hundred meters from the ground!

K.T also looked up and accidentally swiped the energy from his hand along the slit in Speedo. K.T was suddenly enclosed in white energy and the armor detached itself from the hovering position and attached on K.T. The arm armor clanged on right after the elbow and before the hand joint. Same went for the other arm. His stomach and waist armor went on. The stomach and waist armor was an all-proof rubber and the pelvis guard was crafted out of lightweight silver and the chest armor had shoulder plates made out of pure but also lightweight gold. T.K's thigh and shin armor banged together and the foot protection was red and shaped like a shoe but iron talons were attached. His helmet went on and twin hatches flipped up and two bars attached over his mouth. In the center was a microphone like thing that served as an air filter and a talk center. A green transparent visor that covered the eyes came down. All of this armor was lightweight but extremely tough and the rest of K.T's body was bare.

He clipped the Speed access to his waist and he climbed out of the pit and ran off.

The armor gave K.T access to speed beyond human limits!!! K.T's speed was equivalent to the speed of supersonic multiplied by 107! Yet it was effortless and totally in control of the speed that the armor channeled into K.T. But all of that control and effortlessness was not visible to other people because K.T was so fast that he looked like a black and yellow blur. He was even nimble enough to run on rapid water!!

"Hey K.T, wherever you are watch out for that big giant stone in your way!!" cried Max, extremely worried.

The macow was going to burn up any second and K.T did not have time to run around the rock cause' the rock was one thousand feet in length and ten thousand feet in diameter. Speedo suddenly told him

"Galactic protector, use your special power that the armor mentally taught you to access!!"

"Okay!!" said K.T. with a lion war cry K.T yelled "Speed Armor! Slow time!!!"

And held out his hand. Time suddenly slowed and it seemed as if this planet was in slow motion!! It slowed everything except K.T and he did a stunning gymnastic! He flipped himself holding the top of the rock with a single hand straight up! Then with the superman strength that the Speed Armor accessed to K.T he curled into a ball and did uncountable flips into the air!! T.K accelerated close enough to the unconscious macow into his arms and released time. K.T sped down but didn't burn because his armor prevented it. When he neared the ground he called upon the Armor to do a slow roll and come up without a scratch! The macow came into conscious again, tested its wing and took off. Diamond, Sarah and Max's jaws all dropped to the ground as they were extremely stunned.

"I made it!!" cried K.T.

"He made it!" cried K.T's friends as they all ran over towards him and warmly embraced him.

Ch 4 The first hints of Evil

In a cave hidden deep beneath the surface of the peaceful planet, serpents hissed and poisonous fungus and mushrooms blew their infecting spores. In the center of the solitary grotto, serpents of all kinds slithered over a group of four muscular men. All tied up with chains made out of silver. The snakes injected their venom as they passed. The men screamed with pain as the poison coursed through their veins. They saw the silhouette of a grotesque figure. Then came a pulling sensation. The last vision that the men saw was a small glowing sphere being absorbed by the dark figure...

K.T was again zipping all over the place, trying to get really used to the incredible speed. He zoomed up and down the highest mountains he could find. He caused rock slides by running on loose rock and calling upon his power to freeze time (he mastered his Armor so much that he earned the ability to freeze time instead of slowing down time) and smash the boulders with his armor strength. All of a sudden K.T accidentally smashed the outer layer of the mountain and found a secret entrance to unknown places. But they did not get a chance to explore the cave because oversized and possessed liontelopes came charging out and started swiping at all of the friends. They all took cover behind large rocks except K.T. he rushed forward, jumped to the liontelope's eye level and *tried* to launch a kick but the oversized creatures had some tricks up their fur too. They roared and the roar was so loud that the sound waves became physical and it even cracked the ground!! Even though K.T's speed was fast the *power* of the roar was better. The overwhelming sound waves got to K.T as he neared the liontelopes, threw him some feet away and knocked him unconscious. Now the others were watching and as the creatures moved in for the kill. Diamond spotted something glowing inside the cave. It was a cube of the same energy that made up the cylinder where the speed armor was floating and Diamond knew it was designated for her.

"Keep the liontelopes distracted!! I'll go for the armor!!" yelled Diamond. The others nodded and set off. Max and Sarah went behind the liontelopes and yelled and jumped up and down.

"Hey you big ugly brutes! Come and get us!!" the hybrids turned and with their attention redirected chased the other two.

Ch 5 The second (but surprising and strange) armor

While Max and Sarah were running like hell and screaming like girls (well Sarah is a girl) from the hybrids Diamond was walking through the cave to the armor, feeling a bit guilty for sending her friends on an almost-suicidal job.

"Huh, this isn't armor, it looks more like an outdated fashion outfit!!!" and it was true! The armor was a hovering cloak dark, dark blue with a jet-black hood but that cloak was ultra durable, harder than diamond and sliver fused together and it was fully flexible. The chest armor was like K.T's but purple with orange lines going across and there was no stomach and waist armor. There was a skirt that was light purple and it was made out of the same material as the cloak. The gloves and boots were also the same material as the skirt and had small emerald spheres on them. The color was for both gloves and boots midnight black. The gloves and boots went to the elbow and knee.

"This is like totally weird, armor that is made out of cloth! Hello? Anyone ever heard of the five billionth century?" Diamond remarked.

"Hurry Diamond, the liontelopes are catching up! Ahhhhhhhhh we are at a barrier of boulders!!" Sarah and Max screamed together.

Diamond found a loose, small, and gleaming silver jewel on the armor, tugged at it and it popped off.

"Greetings, the second Galactic Protector. I am the Shadow access jewel. You may refer to me as Black Angel."

It said in a misty voice and it launched a beam of black energy with a thin green aura around it at Diamond's left hand. Instead of the energy that energized the cube, a black with an orange aura orb surrounded her hand. Diamond then held both hands up, a single hand griping the jewel and the other hand the energy pulsed. When the jewel and the energy met, black electricity shot out of the orb and zapped Diamond. The flesh of Diamond absorbed the electricity and unleashed her inner strength. The armor then slipped itself on diamond without any noise. Diamond placed the jewel on her head and it stuck firmly.

She rushed out and activated her power. She transformed invisible, only her shadow remained. Diamond ran invisibly over to where the liontelopes were going to swipe the guts out of Max and Sarah and she stomped on the feet of the liontelopes. The armor also gave her the strength of an elephant. The two hybrids snarled in pain and *tried to see* who stomped on their feet but all they saw was their own feet. Black Angel spoke to Diamond in her mind using telepathy.

"Activate your special power." It said.

Diamond held out her hands and concentrated. Her eyes turned red and her hands made a net of the black energy that powered her. Using all her mental strength she hurled the net without exerting her physical force. The net snared the first liontelope and it soothed it. The possessing force went out of the body and the liontelope shrank back to its normal size.

"So it wasn't oversized after all." Remarked Max. The evil spirit made an attempt to escape but with a

"Oh no, you won't flee." From Diamond and a black orb encased it, immobilizing the spirit's movement.

To de-possess the second liontelope Diamond launched a series of kicks and punches just with a black force ahead of them.

"Shadow spinning kick! Shadow uppercut! And Shadow bolt!!" she cried as Diamond shot a bolt of shadow energy!

That subdued the liontelope by knocking it unconscious. K.T just regained conscious and saw the evil possessing spirit flee.

"Stop, you won't stop I'll just have to force you! Speed Armor, stop time!!" K.T cried as he held out his hand.

The spirit instantly froze and K.T was able to trap it in a jar.

"Whoever sent those spirits was trying to kill us, someone who doesn't want peace on this planet."

"This might be a coincidence but if someone perhaps is trying to kill us..." Started Sarah.

"Let's move on." said Max while Diamond and K.T withdrew their armor into their Accesses.

"What is the rush, we have plenty of time." Asked Sarah.

"I'm not in a hurry to run into a monster that is possessed." Said Max, walking faster.

Nightfall…

Ch 6 Troubled night...

"Okay! Let's make a camp for the night and one of us will have to stand guard while we sleep." Said Sarah

"I suffer from insomnia so I would love to guard the camp at the dead of the night." said K.T.

While the others were placing their efforts in lighting a burning fire Diamond was out hunting nourishment for them because everyone ate their remaining food on the long, two week trek to the edge of the border of the Nightmare Mountains. It was not very eventful for it was just desert with the occasional sandstorm.

Not much vegetation or wildlife flourished around the border so Diamond's exhausted feet carried her to a small group of wolf rat. It resembled a rat but a meter high it was. Instead of buck teeth, they had gleaming and super sharp fangs. Also its spiky fur was useful for getting bodies healthy. Diamond spotted an extremely plump one and caught it in an orb of black energy where it commenced to suffocate. The flames were roaring a cheery orange and red as the wolf rat cooked. The team got gloomy as they thought about their parents at home missing them and wondering if their teacher, Ms. Dinklebutt, had told them off for not being at school for **_last 2 Days of school_** and missing the ultra important exam. She might have already expelled them for she hated the four of them and conducted every scheme in the book to get them in trouble. Examples are, dragging them off to the principal's office because she found brownies in their lunches and it was a school rule, "No sweets are allowed." How she found out, she looked through their backpacks. (This is very rude for a teacher to do). Another example is making them late for class by tripping them in the hallway and while they are getting up, she kicks their books right up to their principal's office and when they walk to retrieve their books, the principal assumes that they had been kicking their own books and gave them detentions and warning and lectures. The irresistible smell of meat roasted to perfection wafted into their noses and knocked them out of their thoughts. The meat **was** juicy, tender and a taste bud knock out!!

"Good thing Diamond found **that** group of wolf rats or we'll be eating buzzaleon liver!" joked Max.

Everyone stuck their tongue out at Max. Sarah suddenly gagged and spat out something at the warm fire. Before it went up in flames, they caught sight of it.

"What was that?!!" they asked altogether.

"Fur ball." answered Sarah.

"Fur ball?!!!" exclaimed Sarah.

"Sarah you're growing hair and whiskers, and you're shrinking!!!" K.T yelled. Sarah was transforming into a cat!

Ch 7 Sarah the cat

"Meow, meow, meow!" shrieked Sarah. Max, who liked to be a tease, shrieked with laughter.

"Hey everyone, Sarah is a cat that resembles her cat, Sarah!!"

Everyone laughed. Sarah was furious. She launched herself at Max and started to slash him. Diamond was the first to recover from laughter. A sphere she formed around the fire and, using her special power to make shadow gloves, she picked through the fire, searching for the essence or substance that transformed Sarah. She made the sphere as though to not wipe out the fire as she was searching.

"Found it!" yelled Diamond and held the burnt pieces up. Everyone leaned closer to view the ashes.

"Meow, meeeow?" as if to say "What is it?"

"Hmmmmm... said K.T (who was always the teacher's pet in science class) it looks like etc..." he began an incredibly boring lecture about the laws of transformation and physical looks and the chemical reactions that would bore even a science geek. While Max looked like he was listening he was actually wondering why only Sarah transformed.

"Just coincidence, or maybe the one who placed the chemical in that leg knew Sarah loved eating legs and he purposely set out that plump one." thought Max.

"I believe someone or something doesn't want Sarah to obtain her armor because right this very instant, her body shape is ill-fitted to wear human sized armor." Said Max interrupting K.T.

"I was about to get to that ,Max, and I believe someone or something doesn't want Sarah to obtain her armor because right this very instant, her body shape is ill-fitted to wear human sized armor." Dawn soon came and the team realized had they had been talking for the whole night and that annoyed the day time animals. All of the animals surrounded our group of friends and ripped and tore them apart without any mercy.

Just kidding

Of course the animals had that in mind and just when they had their feet planted on the ground, waiting to spring, Sarah stepped in front of them and purred and made a really cute face. That cleared the animals' minds and they stood on the spot, immobilized by the cuteness and savoring the glory of getting to view Sarah in her cute postures. That kept them distracted while the others snuck away. Finally Sarah, cutely, asked them to leave. The animals obeyed without question

Ch 8 Aw man, more fighting

K.T was again zipping and zagging as he trained to perfect his control of the armor. Diamond was also breaking mountains with her crushing and powerful shadow wielding power. Also she was playing tricks on the team by turning invisible and poking them when they least expect it. Sarah was cat-napping in the warmth of, not the Sun but Novaguva, the star that heated and lit up Planet Mythical Peace. Max was sitting beside Sarah, bored out of his pants.

"Look, I'm going to go explore this planet." He said.

"You'll be liontelope dinner if you don't have an armor!" said K.T

"The armor is for knocking out baddies, wherever they are, not wild animals!" Max called back.

5 minutes later...

"AHHHHHHHHHHHHHHHHHHH!" screamed Max as he sped back to the camp while a pair possessed elephaboonbas tore after him.

But the elephaboonbas were not possessed by evil spirits sent from the now ruthless Emperor of Serpents that wanted to kill the team but he installed twin mind controlling devices on the heads of the elephaboonba and fed them trans-mutant-morphagu potions that made them mutants and dangerous. They now had blue fur, freezing breath and blazing heat vision, spikes jutting out of the back, a huge tail with a bone club at the end. Eyes were a gleaming blood red, and as the mutants swished their bronze and iron trunks Max, K.T, Sarah, and Diamond could see gnashing teeth, T. rex teeth. "Armor, stop time!!" cried K.T.

"Meow meow meow." This meant "Okay whoever is good at hacking electronics, step forward." Said Sarah.

Everyone took a big step back and Sarah was in front.

"Meow." This meant "Fine."

"Shadow Bonds!!" cried Diamond as her hand palms released eight large rings formed out of Shadow power. The rings snapped the mutant elephanboonba's legs together so when Sarah neared the mutants and unsheathed her claws the trampling feet won't crush her.

"Time for distractions." Said K.T, smiling and he was off!

Zigging and zagging across the elephanboonba's line of vision he did. The mutant elephanboonba were dumber than the real ones because the Trans-mutant-morphagu potion filled the brain with toxins and blocked all the sections of the brain except the body functions and anger. Now the elephanboonba were getting seriously annoyed and *tried* to lumber toward K.T but tripped over the Shadow bonds and crashed right in front of Sarah. The mutants were temporarily unconscious and Sarah made her move. She pounced lightly on one of the elephanboonba's backs, careful to avoid the spikes and unsheathed her claws and unlocked the hatch.

Ch.9 Mistress of Weapons and the cure to the fur

"Meowwwwwww." This meant,

"My god, this is even more complex than the computers that I've hacked before when I was human to stop robberies, and they had security devices!!"

"Then just smash it!!" yelled Max and picked up a large rock and threw it at the exposed wires and software.

The rock collided with the controls with such force that it exploded!! Sarah was hit by a large bottle of

Trans-mutant-morphagu that just blasted out of the controls before it blew.

"Me-owwwwwwwwwwww!!!!!!" hissed Sarah as she flew backwards. Suddenly the still-mutant elephanboonba eyes suddenly glowed a fierce bright red and went on a rampage!

"I believe that just after its mind-controlling device was destroyed there was a shock wave that occurred in the mind and damaged something." Said K.T, backing away slowly.

"Will it heal?" asked Diamond nervously.

"Yes but in the meantime…"

"Incoming! Crazed and mutant elephanboonba rampage coming at twelve-o clock!!" yelled Max who was running like hell and in left arm a fainted Sarah. In his right hand was a bottle of Trans-mutant-morphagu potion that was a khaki color of boogers.

"Shadow Confusion Attack!!!! Diamond as the combined strength of her mind and her Power Armor she launched a volley of lemon yellow spheres with black spheres inside.

"What did you do?!!" asked Max as the spheres collided with the elephanboonba and they commenced to fight each other.

"I used a Shadow Confusion Attack to confuse the elephanboonba into thinking that each other is an enemy."

"A good tactic, but with one flaw…"

Started K.T and Max finished it.

"One of your "spheres" hit the remaining device and the rest of the attack all froze thanks to their icy breath and now they are … furious!!!!!!!!!!!" "Oops." Said Diamond meekly with a worried look on her face.

The mutants charged.

"Look out!!" cried K.T and accidently knocked the bottle of Trans-mutant-morphagu potion and Sarah out of Max's hands. The potion hit the ground first and smashed. Sarah came a second later and landed *right in the remains of the smashed potion!!* The force of the impact woke her up and as she rasped of oxygen she drank a bit of the potion!!

"Ewwwwwwwwwwwwwwwwww!! This stuff is nasty and…" "Hey I'm human again!!" exclaimed Sarah. She pressed a button on her mecha watch and a hatch popped open and a mirror flipped itself out.

"I'm normal… except for my eyes and my teeth. My eyes used to be blue but now they are blood red and my front teeth are sharper."

"Look, the third armor…" Started K.T but was cut off by Max.

"Yeah, my armor, I'm getting bored of watching you use Armors." And took a run at the glowing pyramid with a wide grin on his face but that turned upside down instantly. Max was shot back the moment he touched the energy and landed hard on the ground. Max was very disappointed. As Sarah walked nervously toward the armor Max's face looked extremely hurt. It was either from getting thrown back from the energy and landing hard or not receiving an armor. Suddenly there was a trumpet-like sound and the team turned around. The mutant elephanboonba had found more mutant elephanboonba and had recruited them to kill the team. Now an entire empire of mutants surrounded the team and lowered their tusks, gnashing their teeth and walked slowly inwards, forcing the team to be back to back. Sarah, being the only one out of the ring of elephanboonbas and closest to the armor, she rushed toward the armor. The armor was exactly shaped like K.T's but it was army camafluage colors and weapons covered it. Grenades surrounded the waist and under the grenades were time bombs and heat-activated mini-bombs. Four medium sized laser blasters were on either side of the waist and a sword whose blade was made out of fire and was retractable was hooked on the left. Twin stun staffs were hooked on the back. As were two long swords, a crystal bow with arrows of werewolf teeth heads and wood of energized prehistoric lilacs which stems were diamond-hard, and there was a drill on a staff. A machine gun that fired plasma blasts with rapid firing madness was attached to the right arm armor. On the left a long and tubular blaster that can be charged and shot electricity. On the bottom of the arm armor, there was a small rocket launcher that also served as a hammer. Dragon skin gloves protected the hands. Also the Weapon Access was the same as K.T's.

"Cool, my armor is a Mistress of Weapons!!" said Sarah.

Ch 10 Mutants and something else is on the loose...

"Ahhhhhhhhhhhhhhhh, Sarah hurry up, we are running out of space the elephanboonbas's tusks are getting closer by the second and we are going to be Swiss cheese!" yelled Max.

Sarah pressed a button on the ipod like thing and it shot the same energy as on K.T's Access. She swiped the energy on the slit. The armor detached itself and joined on Sarah.

"Nice, these weapons were weapons I could only dream of handling!!" said Sarah.

"Use them now!!!!!" cried the team.

Sarah grabbed eight mini detonators, four in each hand and threw them. Her aim was true and they attached themselves on eight mutant elephanboonbas. Sarah pressed a button on her arm armor and yelled

"Fire in the hull!!!" and the detonators blew. That killed ten elephanboonba but suddenly a giant army of evil buzzaleons the size of blue whales came charging down mountains and the team saw that they had been mutated by the Trans-mutant-morphagu too. Their eyes glowed a furiously vivid purple, their stingers now had the ability to launch the stingers filled with venom and they could reload. Also their tail was divided into triple tails and they were scorpion tails. Their front teeth were enlarged to saber like fangs, top and bottom. The mutants had forelegs of armadillo and hind legs of an elephant and its frill was permanently spread. Also at the end of the mouth, after the saber-teeth there was a super strong beak of an eagle. Its breath was a semi-transparent rainbow beam which would not do any harm but would weaken the enemy so badly that they would be defenseless against the second beam; a beam of forceful water with electricity encircling it. Now the team had two troubles to deal with.

"I'll handle the mutant buzzaleon, you guys take on the elephanboonba!" said Sarah.

"Okay!" the rest said together.

"Here, Max take this, now you can fight too." Said Sarah as she threw the flame sword at him. He caught it. The fight was on. Max ignited the flame sword the second he caught it and started fighting. Sarah threw more detonators and they hit dead on. The explosion force knocked Sarah off her feet and vulnerable to a beam of the weakness blast fired by another buzzaleon. While Sarah was struggling to regain her energy Max was trying to find an opening to slash his sword. Meanwhile the elephanboonba he was fighting was stomping its mighty feet and breathing its icy breath.

"Little help please."

Max yelled to K.T as the ice breath froze the fiery blade.

"I'm a little busy right now, can't go!" said K.T as he kicked and confused the elephanboonba. The kicks to the head knocked the elephanboonba unconscious instantly so he was careful to strike the head. Diamond was the one to come to Max's aide. Her powers snared the advancing elephanboonba with a Shadow net. After that she launched a storm of Shadow balls to hit the rest of elephanboonbas.

"Yeah!!" they all cried as Diamond, Max and K.T all did a high five.

"Back!! Stay back, I'm warning you."

They all turned and saw Sarah using her stun staffs, still too weak to reach her guns but keeping the buzzaleons at bay with her weapons.

"Take this buzzaleons!!!!" yelled Max and threw the frozen flame sword at the eye of the buzzaleon. His hit was a bulls-eye and the buzzaleon was blinded long enough for Sarah to recover. She said

"Diamond, lend me some Shadow power."

Diamond obeyed, puzzled and released a sphere of Shadow power which Sarah fused with her long swords and they became laser long swords. She raised the sword and swung it hard on the ground.

"Energized long sword fissure blast!!" yelled Sarah

The ground burst as rainbow energy went and disintegrated anything in the way of the energy. Most of the buzzaleons were killed but a few survived and shot their beam of energy to weaken.

"Hey wait here, I have and idea guys." Said K.T

He ran round and round in a circle and a mini dust twister rose.

"Hit the dust tornado with some shadow balls, Diamond!! Said K.T

"Got it K.T." said Diamond

And she threw a few Shadow balls and the dust tornado became a Shadow tornado. The moment the rainbow beam hit the Shadow tornado it rebounded and hit their owners. Now the buzzaleons were the ones that were weak and Max finished them off with a laser blaster that Sarah gave him and told him he could keep it. Now I have to warn you of an extremely unfortunate event that followed so brace yourselves. A flood of flames suddenly came and surrounded the team and burned them to cinders.

Just kidding☺☺

Well they would if it weren't K.T's speed and as the fires closed in he grabbed all of his friends and rushed out of the fire. The fires raced after them as if it was homing fire. They ran halfway around the planet and when they reached the grave lands the fire had died out and the team was in the middle of nowhere, and the worst part is that the Nightmare Mountains were on the other side of the planet!!

"Ohhhhhhhhhhhhh… I don't feel so good…" said K.T as he threw up because of the putrid air.

"K.T that is just nasty!!!" said Sarah, looking away.

"I can't help it the air here is really putrid!!" answered K.T.

"Guys why don't we go back and find some Blue Nectar to purify this dump!" said Max.

"Great idea Max, but with one flaw, the fire burned everything!!!" said Sarah sadly.

"And to make matters worse, a huge spider mech is headed our way!!!!" cried Diamond.

Ch 11 Max's powerful armor

That spider mech was designed to be like a spider but made of titanium, diamond, and orichalkos (a really powerful rock that the Atlanteans, people of Atlantis used to build). The head and abdomen were shielded with plasma. But the legs were vulnerable against attack.

"Let's go!!" said K.T and they all unleashed their armor. Sarah threw eight plasma grenades. They hit the legs and she yelled

"Fire in the hull!" and the grenades blew.

"That finished him." Said Max.

"Not yet!" yelled K.T

Out of the smoke the spider mech rushed out, raised its forelegs and pounded hard on the ground. The shock waves from the pounding knocked the team flat on their backs. The mech suddenly launched a bolt of plasma that would incinerate them if Diamond didn't have a say in this. She used her Shadow power to create a shield from the plasma. As if in retaliation the mech increased the intensity of the plasma and Diamond's shield was shattered. The force of the Shadow shield bursting was a colossal tank ramming into her. She was thrown backwards and landed headfirst into the hard earth and got knocked unconscious. K.T was next. He held out his hand and yelled

"Speed Armor, stop time!"

And was planning to destroy the legs once the mech was frozen but that annoying mech had some tricks up his sleeves too. The plasma shielding was Time-proof. The moment the "Time freezing" touched it rebounded and hit K.T. Now K.T was frozen and the mech launched a beam of plasma that blasted K.T to a boulder. It shattered the moment K.T hit and buried him; of course he was okay but black and red with bruises and cuts.

"Ow, my head…" said K.T.

Sarah launched plasma shot after plasma shot and detonators after detonators but still couldn't break the shield. Sometimes she hit the legs but it seemed to barely harm it. But one leg was destroyed after a successive blast of electricity. All of a sudden a sphere of plasma rushed out at Sarah. She dodged it, but barely. The mech launched a volley of plasma spheres. Sarah evaded all of them. Soon she had to land, right on the abdomen of the spider mech. She could smell burning metal and with haste jumped off. The mech was expecting something like that. It trapped Sarah in its titanium fangs and unleashed a plasma beam. That blew her high in the air and collided with a tree. Now the mech advanced towards Max who was without an Armor and only with a laser blaster. Now I am sorry to leave you on that part which you are all in suspense and waiting to see what happened to Max but first close the book and wait one hour. That should build your suspense. If you ignore this, it is either that you have bad eyesight (No offence if you do) or you are disrespectful of the text of this book!!!

Well here it is, the moment you've all been waiting for... Max shot blasts from the laser blaster he had and it only bounced off the mech's plasma shield. Even if he hit the legs, the laser still didn't harm it because it was too weak. Max ducked and saw the plasma container.

"I need to get under it to destroy its plasma container." Thought Max.

So he raced to the underside of the mech (crouched down) and reached it. He fired his blaster on the exposed inner wiring and software in the hatch he just opened. Suddenly the plasma lasers on the mech were disabled but the spider mech raised itself and launched itself on the ground. Max was going to be crushed but he kept on telling himself

"Be brave, be brave, be brave..."

And he kept on shooting. The mech still slammed hard on the ground but not on Max, at the very last second he jumped into the hatch and was safe. Max was thinking

"Whew, that was way too close!"

The mech, on the other hand, its weapons were un-functional for Max had killed all the wires and broke all the software. Something caught Max's eye and he descended from the mech and found that a Power armor had materialized out of nowhere! Can you guess why it appeared, I left a clue. But the armor was only a helmet the exact shape for a werewolf colored green and blue. Also there were crossing chains the perfect size for a werewolf chest. In the middle a black orb was fixed onto a circular container and on the orb and glowing red the Chinese symbol for "moon". The helmet only covered the top half of a werewolf head and a sword blade made out of harder than diamond moonstone, a hilt of gold and a handle of emerald, there was a fire opal just at the top of the hilt in the blade, the moonstone was constructed by dwarves and it could cut through anything.

"OH COME ON!! My head won't fit, unless I squash it. Oh well, I try it." Said Max

Max held out his hand. Suddenly Max's eyes glowed bright yellow and he transformed into a werewolf with the power of speech and control. The armor attached itself on and Max was suited up. He howled. All of a sudden the weather became freezing cold and the full moon was out. A dozen arctic wolves appeared out of nowhere and started attacking the mech. The mech was sluggish now because most of its controls were destroyed. Max, as a werewolf drew his moonstone sword and sliced off all the legs. The rest of the body was frozen. Max now lowered his hand and the weather conditions became normal and the wolves disappeared. His friends started to wake up and saw Max just transforming back into human.

"Wow, Max your armor is werewolf?!" asked K.T

"Not just werewolf, I have control over myself and the power of speech too! Also I can summon arctic wolves to attack, control the moon and ice, and I have an enchanted sword!" said Max.

"That is sooooooooooo cool!!!!!!!" said Diamond.

"Hey, what is that in that spider mech?" asked Sarah

They all looked. A hatch had opened and inside was papers that contained some ominous information…

Ch 12 the Emperor of Serpents

"This Emperor of Serpents sounds like a jerk. Imagine killing people just for life force and their muscles!!" said Max.

They were reading the papers and found out that the Emperor of Serpents was a dead man but he was alive but his skin was gone and only his dried muscles remained. His internal organs were gone and his head was a bear skull in front but the back was snake skull. His stomach part was stripped but only a spine and a few muscles remained. Also his right hand was replaced by a bone scythe. In his waist area four snakes have emerged and two snakes wrapped themselves around his legs.

"I wonder how he got himself killed." Said Sarah.

"Probably something fatal, like a long fall or something." Said K.T.

"Guys, said Max, in the movies and T.V after we defeat the enemy the planet or whatever is destroyed is purified and restored!!!!"

"Yeah like that'll work." Said Diamond rolling her eyes

"I have watched many movies, and it has always worked!!" protested Max.

"Look it is nightfall, let's sleep. We need our energy." Said Sarah

"Who's turn to keep watch? Asked K.T

"Mine." Said Diamond

1:00am …

"Everyone wake up! Huge snake headed our way!!" cried Diamond as she shook everyone awake.

"No… let me sleep." Mumbled Max.

"Whoa!! The Emperor of Serpents is on the snake's back!! Yelled K.T

"What?!" yelled Max as he quickly got to his feet.

The Emperor of Serpents was just like the papers said. Only a few things were left out. He was dripping blood all over, his ribs were showing, the snakes were sprouting from a hole in the waist, and his stomach innards were ripped out and…

"That is just sick!!! Stop the narration!! Yelled Max.

"Yeah and those are all insults to me!" yelled the Emperor of Serpents.

"How did you get killed and mutated?" asked K.T

"Well I got killed by falling off a high cliff chasing… a rabbit on this planet."

The team all burst out laughing.

"Anyway I came here as a grown man with a guide that had been here before and the rabbit was really cute so a chased it and fell off a cliff. I was stabbed and ripped by the jagged rocks on the mountain as I fell and dropped into the grotto. There I was healed by the mushroom and fungus spores but my head was ripped off by a snake. But other snakes injected their venom in me and that gave me snake power. After I had enough venom in my body to keep me alive but my muscles were too weak as they were ripped. And then you know the rest from the papers."

"But why destroy this planet?" asked Diamond

"Destroying this planet will cause an explosion that will eliminate all man kind and the universe! Then I will absorb the remains and create a new universe and create new planets to rule and evil creatures to dominate the planets, muahahahahahahahahahahahahahaha!!!"

"Alright enough talk, let's battle to the end!!!" yelled Sarah, not even aware of what she was saying. The others looked somber.

"Wolves, go!!!" yelled Max as wolves appeared out of thin air and began attacking the huge snake.

"Nara echi noxi kahola, Nara echi noxi kahola." The Emperor of Serpents said as that was a magic spell.

The reverse of the reverse spell, a spell that reversed the coldness into flames and the wolves into tyrannosauruses under his control.

"Get them!!"

The dinos obeyed. They ran toward the team. Sarah threw detonator after detonator but the Emperor kept on chanting the reverse of the reverse spell so her detonators went back at her and blew. The explosion threw Sarah to a tree and it knocked her out. Max was having more luck but just barely and with each tyrannosaur he cut two more grew back because the reverse of the reverse spell. K.T was already frozen from his reversed time attack and Diamond was having a competition of mind power for the Shadow sphere she formed around her had begun to shrink from the spell but she was fighting to enlarge it. Now the Serpent king (Emperor of Serpents) had begun chanting a new hex.

"Umo ichi bushu e, umo ichi bushu e."

That was the Hex of Confusion. So now Max accidentally bonked himself on the head with the flat side of his sword, K.T was already frozen and Diamond had blacked out from the stress of holding the Shadow sphere or the hex making her lose her focus.

"Ha! These weaklings are the protectors of this planet!" gloated the Emperor of Serpents.

"Who are you calling weaklings!!" Said a familiar voice.

Max was up, and full of rage. His anger danced in his yellow eyes.

"How did you wake up?!!! Asked the Serpent king.

"I am a werewolf in armor mode so I have tougher skulls and I have this helmet!! Now, I will destroy you, in a sword battle!!" said Max.

"Bring it on!" said the Serpent king.

He drew his Serpentall sword made by the snake god himself and launched himself at Max.

"Argggggggggh!!" cried Max as the Serpent king's hand scythe slashed his chest.

Max made a wild slash with his sword but the Serpent king was too quick. He dodged and using his sword he made a deep wound in Max's left arm and brought the sword up take slice the head. Max parried the blow but suddenly the Serpent king's foot launched a kick with the force of a rampaging football player to Max's stomach. Max was on his knees and the Emperor of Serpents was laughing.

"Ahahahahahahahahahahahahahaha, give me your armor, and I'll spare your life."

"Never!!" yelled Max

"So be it, die!!!!" yelled the Serpent king as he swung his sword down.

Max jumped at the last second and his jaws bit down on the ribs of the Serpent king…

Max's jaws closed on the ribs, he was determined to harm the Serpent king in all the ways, crushing his ribs and ripping out his heart and lungs was one of them.

"Ah, get off me you savage werewolf!!"

"I am a savage werewolf you moron!!" yelled Max and with those words Max became a full-fledged werewolf. The chains broke and his helmet was discarded. His teeth were sharper and that was perfect for crushing the ribs but…

Now I am sure that you are thinking that Max will tear up the Emperor of Serpents limb from limb and the Planet Mythical peace will be purified and the team will leave and live happily ever after. Sorry that is not it.

But the Serpent king threw a punch and knocked Max unconscious. He dragged his unconscious victims away. His horrible laugh echoed through the night, sending all of the animals into their dens.

Ch 13 Prisoners...

"Oh where are we…" asked Max groggily.

He was bound to the wall of a cave with some kind of strange magical field. Whenever Max tried to disperse it, he was forcefully zapped.

"We are in the Serpent king's lair, just like a movie. For five days!" Said K.T

"Yeah like in the movie *Spies*. The spies infiltrate the enemy base and get captured and somehow manage to escape and blow up the enemy base." Said Sarah.

"Well you aren't going to blow up my base." Said the Emperor of Serpents.

"We'll find a way." Said Max confidently.

"Well then I wish you happy plotting because I have the Staff of the Ancient Serpent gods at my command so my magical power has increased by 7 thousand."

"Nice, real smooth. Now what?" asked Diamond.

"Find his weakness." Said K.T

"How, his powers are far greater than us combined!" wailed Sarah.

"I think I have found his weakness, look at what he is crooning over." Said Max

They all craned their heads to look. There the Serpent king was, spoiling a rabbit, the very rabbit that led him to his doom.

"You worship a rabbit?!!!" said Max.

"Yes." Answered the Emperor of Serpents.

"Well, we can take it and suffocate it, unless we bargain." Said K.T

"Alright, what do you want." Said the Serpent king as Diamond grabbed the rabbit using Shadow power and made a Shadow ring around its neck.

"Freedom." Said Sarah.

"Deal."

Just as the field disappeared the Emperor of Serpents yelled

"Psyche!!!"

And cobras flew from his fingertips. They wrapped themselves firmly around the team. Satisfied, the Serpent King slammed his Staff into the ground and it began to crack.

"You're honored, you get to see the destruction of this planet from front row seats!" shouted the Emperor of Serpents.

Max wasn't going to let this planet become annihilated without a fight! So he let out a howl and transformed into a full-fledged werewolf but now with more improvements. He had a belt of moonstone and silk made from dwarves made to chain the savage and humungous wolf Fenrir. It was made from the breath of a salmon, tear of a Hercules beetle, scale of an elephant and the eye of a god. His eyes were now a gleaming red and on his back was the Chinese symbol for moon. He wrenched his muscular limbs up and ripped the snakes. Then he freed his friends from the serpents. Max threw his body into the Emperor of Serpents, knocking his Staff of the Ancient Serpent Gods from his hand onto the ground.

"You're arrogant, Serpent king!!" Max yelled.

"Oh yeah?!!" said the Serpent king as he chanted a new jinx. The jinx of power absorbing but suddenly Max shouted.

"I summon the spirits of the Nidhogg (a dragon with stag antlers) and Fenir (a giant wolf)!! Vanquish the evil!!"

From Max's furry hand a blue spirit of the Nidhogg and a black spirit of Fenir materialized. They both launched themselves at the Emperor of Serpents, Nidhogg flying fast and Fenir running and pounced, both jaws open wide. "Don't you see what you are doing?!! You are tapping into the most powerful evil, the summoning of the evil spirits that fought in Ragnarok!" yelled the Serpent king as the spirits rushed towards him.

"Evil spirits..." twitched K.T, Sarah, and Diamond.

"I can handle them!" yelled Max even though he looked like he was going to pass out.

"Noooooooooooooooo!!" yelled the Emperor of Serpents as the spirits hit.

The spirits disintegrated the Emperor of Serpents and there was a humungous explosion and the team was blasted off their feet over halfway across the planet and just a few miles away from the Mountains of Fire and Shadow!!

"Well what do you know; we did kill his base, just like the movies *Spies* but only in reality." Said Diamond confidently.

K.T smelled the air, expecting refreshing and clean air but instead he smelled rotting flesh and pollution. That made K.T barf again.

"K.T, that looks like the Serpent king's heart, only wetter and mushier." Complained Sarah

"Hey, the land is not purified yet, that means...

The Serpent king isn't dead!!!" yelled Diamond

Ch 14 Armor, Spirit, and Body X Fusion

"Max, are you sure that your power was enough to destroy the Serpent king? … Max?" asked Sarah.

They all turned to look at Max just in time to see a cobra spirit go inside him. His body shuttered for a moment and stopped. When he spoke his voice was not his, it was the voice of the Emperor of Serpents!!

"Max has tapped too much into the panel of darkness and made him vulnerable for me to possess. I chose him because he is the strongest of you all."

"What will we do? We can't fight Max, it'll damage him." Said Diamond.

Max all of a sudden threw himself at his friends, gave three quick jabs and punches and body-checked all of them.

"I'm not finished yet! I summon the Spirit from Tartarus, Kronos!!!"

Kronos was an evil titan and his spirit was a spinning ball of darkness and it was launched.

"Then we will summon a god to counter-attack! Pool all your strength to summon... Zeus, the king of gods!!" the team yelled together, held out their hands and joined them. With a war cry they all converted their strength, armor and mind, into summoning the Ruler of the Heavens.

"We summon the spirit from the Heavens... Zeus!!

Suddenly a lightning bolt flew out of their hands. That was the spirit of Zeus.

"We will teach you real power, as a team!!!" K.T, Sarah, and Diamond yelled.

Now that is a popular phrase when the heroes is about to beat the stuffing out of the villains. Okay back to the story.

The thunderbolt and the ball of the darkness met and there was an explosion that knocked the spirit of the Emperor of Serpents out of Max's body.

"Fools, just because I don't have a solid object to possess doesn't mean that I can't get rid of this world!" yelled the spirit.

"Oh... my head... I don't remember anything..." groaned Max.

"We must get rid of the spirit of the Serpent king once and for all!

"I know what to do, said Diamond; try to merge ourselves into one!! That'll make us strong enough to blow the spirit right out of this planet!! I saw that in a cartoon and it destroyed all the evil in the world!"

"Okay." Said the rest of the team.

"Armor, Spirit, Body X Fusion!!" they all cried and suddenly there was an outburst of light. The outline of four figures suddenly merged into one. When the light subsided, the team was one. It was a fusion of all the Armors.

It had Max's werewolf body to wear the armor. K.T's leg pads, arm pads, and chest armor. For Diamond's Armor the hooded cloak, (the hood was gone though, so it was just a cape) stayed and the gloves stayed too but were only to the end of the hand. Fire was flaming on the thighs and that gave the fusion extra speed and protection. Sarah's weapons stayed and the pelvis guard and waist armor were on. There were some new features like Max's tail had a spiked bone club at the end, on his back was a Chinese symbol for moon dragon. Max's face was Fenir's face, and last but not least there was a super durable sapphire orb with the image a howling wolf in the center of the chest armor. Also a fist made of diamond and gold and it was super hard on the right hand. It could even smash mountains and cause earthquakes! It was named the Fist of the Dragon of Ra Ex.

"We are one." Said a voice that was the combined of the team's voices.

"We understand now, the dragon chose us because we had good friendship and passed the test of summoning the spirit of Zeus. That proved that we are the chosen ones to save the planet from total annihilation!"

"Now, it is time to eliminate all the darkness and purify this planet!!!"

The fusion all of a sudden grew very large and strong wings of an Archaeopteryx, a prehistoric feathered bird. It made a fist and held it Superman style with the left arm down. The fist was now glowing bright yellow.

"Ultimate Dragon Punch of the Ancient Power Armors!!!" Yelled the fusion.

The punch made contact with the spirit and it blew. Suddenly an atomic explosion went under the Fusion. The fusion watched as the atomic particles raced across the planet, purifying the land. All the animals were restored. The mutants were changed back into their normal form. There was another explosion. It seems that the Mountains of Shadow and Fire were no more for the Emperor of Serpents' evil had been vanquished. The fusion then flew back down to Planet Mythical Peace and split. The team was all in their human form and still kept the armor. Max's armor now fused with his body. He could now change into a full-fledged werewolf. When he was that he had Fenir's head, partly human hands (furry), and the rest of him was a normal werewolf and didn't have to wear armor and a Chinese symbol for moon was on his head, also he had ~~speed~~ the speed of sound, strength of an elephant, and ice breath. Actually, I made a mistake that is a lot of difference!

"Wow, Diamond where did you get such an idea?!!" asked Max

"Just watch all the T.V shows, it will give you ideas." Answered Diamond

"But the Nightmare Mountains are destroyed!! Along with our only means of going back to Earth." cried K.T

"I wouldn't say that if I were you K.T." Said a voice.

Ch 15 Earth's destruction

They all looked and saw that the dragon that carried them here was back.

"I can't believe I had to wake up from my slumber, I was just having an incredible dream about luxury… anyway, to the point. The Earth is going to burn up from the sun in a couple of hours and we need to evacuate the planet and bring them here. My body can hold all of Earth's population." It said.

"Okay." Replied the team and the dragon changed back into a subway train.

"I know a spell that will bring all the buildings and animals from Earth to here." Said Diamond and she chanted the spell of teleportation. Suddenly all the buildings, animals, famous landmarks, everything until Earth was left flat, were transported from there to Planet Mythical Peace.

"Hurry, the Earth is going to be incinerated by the Sun in one hour!!" yelled the dragon.

"How fast can you fly around the Earth under the condition that some people will need persuading." Asked Diamond.

"About 57 minutes." Answered the dragon.

"You guys go ahead, said K.T; I need to ensure that no one poaches any of the animals. And, wait, you're the one that attacked the macow so I could find the Armor! "

"Sure, and you guessed it. Good job K.T." And off the dragon flew (back in subway form).

"Wait! I have something else to ask you!" K.T. yelled but it was too late. The Dragon had already flown off. The great dragon flew through the hyperspace and back to Earth. They saw that the Sun had already killed Mercury and Venus and was headed for Earth. First they went to Europe. That continent was easy to persuade because all the people had been expecting the heat of the sun because they had good scientists. Also, when they heard that they can live another day, all of the population rushed into the subway immediately. The team was shocked. Asia was a lot more difficult because the people had not been warned and sometimes, even when they explained the situation, they had to say

"Do you want to live another day?"

Asia was evacuated. In Australia, since the city population was warned, the team had to actually drag the aboriginals into the train since they didn't know how to speak their language. In Antarctica the people were into the subway right after the children explained the situation. In North America, no trouble because of the excellent scientists and in South America… trouble. Almost none wanted to leave their precious Earth, even if they were going to die. So to persuade them they said that there will be plenty of similarities between the two worlds and all the world's animals will be there and all of the population of the world will be there. That made them think about it and finally they agreed. The sun was drawing closer and closer. They flew out of earth's atmosphere and if they left anyone the dragon took a deep breath and sucked up anyone left behind on Earth. Max then (in werewolf mode) froze the Earth and with one final look at the home planet that supported life for trillions of years, off they flew and an explosion sounded after them. Earth was gone forever.☹

Ch 16 The new life

Through the Hyperspace they flew and arrived at Planet Mythical Peace, just like what happened a month and a half back.

When they landed all of Earth's population was befuddled by the air and the team saw that K.T had just came running towards his parents who were all worried sick. They also observed that the land had been divided into countries, just like on Earth. They asked K.T what he did to the animals.

"Oh, I collared them with a high tech and edible band and the band will detect any weapon or anything that can do damage them and it can't be fooled. I also have four hand beepers for each of us. If it beeps really loudly that means a poacher, someone that's helping poachers, or man made weapon or trap is near. If it sings a song it means it is hunted by a wild animal."

"But what if we are sound asleep?" asked Sarah.

"I can go to the rescue, remember I told you guys that I have insomnia and I sleep lightly." Answered K.T.

They all hugged warmly and gathered the population of Earth for a conference. They first got a language megaphone which when they talked the people who are listening will hear their number one language.

"People of Earth, Max said, this conference is to pass laws of this planet. They are all the same laws on Earth but be warned, those who try to murder us, even when we are asleep, we will know and if you try to unnecessarily chop down trees too."

The next day…

"NO!! You are not allowed to enter this school's grounds anymore, you were expelled!!"

They were in the principal's secretary's office.

"Fine, then we won't come, let's use all the time we spend at school exploring more of this planet and having adventures! Said Max.

"Good choice Max, or else we would be spending another year in Mrs. Dincklebutt's company!!" said K.T.

All of them laughed as they walked away from the school.

K.T. suddenly looked as if he realized something. He loked at Diamond, blushing.

"What?" Diamond asked.

"Wait, it is Valentine's Day today. So wanna, uh, hang out Diamond?" K.T asked, blushing.

"Sure." Said Diamond, giggling.

"Will you be my Valentine, Sarah?" asked Max, with a hint of embarrassment in his voice.

"Yes, I'd love to." Replied Sarah smiling and blushing furiously.

Suddenly without explanation Novaguva shone like it never shone before. ☺

Diamond and K.T went to the amusement park. And K.T won a big and grand teddy bear for his Valentine and she gave K.T a kiss on the cheek in gratitude.

Sarah and Max's date was more compassionate. They took a walk beside the stream, holding hands and gazing at the beauty of Nature and each other. Also, they would sit for a few hours on a bench to chat and tease lightly. A kiss on the cheek from Sarah to Max was made when they had to go home.

And so, after Valentine's Day, as promised they had many adventures together. Sometimes they tunneled deep underground using the drill that Sarah had in her armor and once found a race of moles and worms intelligent enough to speak English and build a whole city underground but idiotic enough to not know how to count the numbers or memorize the alphabet, even the old and young people!!

At the school…

"What do you mean that you loathed Diamond, K.T, Sarah and Max?!!" yelled the principal

Mrs. Dincklebutt was in so much trouble, she was in the principle's office and she was being yelled at.

"Well Sir I…

"Well what? Why do hate those kids?"

"I don't know…"

"Well then you're fired!!! You have no right to be a teacher if you don't know!!"

"Aw man…"

Mrs. Dincklebutt was swearing as she left the school grounds and became a hot dog seller for a living. The kids however were having the time of their lives as they destroyed all the remaining evil on the planet like giant demonic peregrine falcons with the Armor, Spirit, Body X fusion. Also in that form they mastered a lot of new techniques like tapping into the Forbidden Arts without doing harm to themselves. Stuff like the summoning the Dark spirits and controlling them. Also they found a cracked orb that belonged to the Serpent king so he could watch the whole planet. They smashed it. At the southern pole of Planet Mythical Peace huge birds that spat sulfuric acid and farted a lot to warn predators that the acid is loaded. The fart was also very stinky. Even with all the peace and no hurricanes, earthquakes, twisters, volcanoes, tsunamis, and all the natural elemental disasters, Diamond still always had an uneasy feeling. Perhaps because she had the shadow armor, that armor had always been the armor that could had a sixth sense or maybe because she was going kookoo. Even when it is not an emergency that they had to go and save people's or animal's lives. It was a feeling like the evil had never been wiped out, even when they disintegrated the last demonic monster on the planet and celebrated by having an enormous party at the Vancouver aquarium. While gazing at the sharks and swimming with the belugas she always felt that way even when she tried to forget it...

Ch 17 Revival of evil

Well Diamond had a right to be nervous because when the team had used the Armor, Spirit, Body X fusion to wipe out the spirit of the Serpent king, it was, well, un-mastered I should say. That caused a fraction of 0.0000000000000000000000001% of weakness that left a microscopic, smaller than the smallest bacteria, even tinier than an atom, piece of the Emperor of Serpents!! So Diamond wasn't going kookoo after all. The leftover particle commenced to float and absorbed power, the radiation from the Armor Spirit Body X fusion and actually got upgraded to his normal form but obtained unnatural powers. He raised his hand and a huge cobra emerged. The Emperor of Serpents leaped on top of it and began chanting a terrible Dark Magic Spell, the spell of Armor Demolition

"Aka telser muchti weara malo demolish!!!!"

Boom!!!!!!!!!!!!!!!!!!!!!!!!!!!!!!!!!! Suddenly the kids were in agony, they were surrounded by a gleaming light and all their Armor were broken apart or transported to different hostile places!! Only Max was unaffected because his Armor was fused.

The next day...

"Well, let's start a quest to find the Armors." Said Sarah

"And I'll try to repair all the armor that was destroyed." Said Max.

"Wait, we need something to protect ourselves with. Who knows what we might encounter." Said Diamond.

"Then we can choose what elemental power we want, my dad has four sacred swords, each containing a different element. Those swords were made before time began and he paid almost $10 million for them" Said K.T

"What elements are there?" asked Sarah

"Earth, water, wind, and fire." answered K.T

"Earth." Said Diamond.

"Water." Said Sarah.

"Fire." Said Max.

"Fine then I choose Wind." Said K.T

"The end... hey this not the end, the digital Narrator has gone insane!! Die digital Narrator!!" yelled the Real Narrator as he grabbed a baseball bat and smashed the fake narrator into spare parts. I know. That was totally random, but I had to put in humor somehow.

A week later…

"Preparations are made and we are ready to go." Said Diamond and the team nodded.

So the intrepid children set off again on their second world saving adventure and walked off to the Nova light.

I know that is a very dramatic scene and ending but I wanted my novel to end really cool so I used it.

To be continued...

Part Two of the New World

Prologue:

Four lucky/unlucky children in the distant future when Earth is at war with aliens, board a supposedly cursed subway train that blasts them off Earth to an unknown and peaceful planet. Along the way the kids locate unique Power Armors that fits each of the kids and channels abilities beyond human control!! But evil is always in the loose just like in every book and movie. The team suffered many difficulties and challenges when trying to rid the land from the dreaded Emperor of Serpents who tried to disintegrate the planet. They succeeded and transported all buildings and landmarks and all of Earth's population to the unknown land. But now, disaster struck. The Emperor of Serpents has been reborn and has destroyed the kids' (except Max's) armor! Now they are on a quest to relocate their missing armor…

Max: Male, twelve years old.
Diamond: female, eleven years old.
K.T: male, nine years old.
Sarah: female, ten years old

Ch 18 Kidnapped

"Look out!!" cried Max as he dove out of the way of a weakness blast shot from a mutant buzzaleon.

"Go, Power Armor!!" yelled Max

Max's body was engulfed with Arctic blue energy. As the energy faded Max was in his werewolf armor. Max grabbed his enchanted moonstone sword and went into a rapid spin. The spin annihilated the buzzaleon but an enormous army of mutant buzzaleons and elephanboonbas waited behind a hill of the seemingly peaceful planet. The mutants bellowed their war cry and charged!

"Quick, everyone grab your elemental blades and do battle!!" Max cried.

The team with elemental blades raised, charged into the fray.

"Earth!!!" yelled Diamond

She slammed her sword into the ground and a giant, magnitude 10 earthquake started. Some mutant elephanboonba lost their balance and knocked a few other mutants into the ground and crushed them.

"Water!!!" yelled Sarah

The remaining elephanboonbas launched a freeze beam and froze the tsunami that Sarah summoned. Suddenly a hurricane tore through the layer of ice and destroyed it.

"Need a hand, or have you got it under control?" asked K.T as he was powering the hurricane.

"Thanks." Answered Sarah.

The tsunami swept away most of the elephanboonba. Max had already killed the buzzaleons by creating a fire wheel (a fire tornado) and launching it. Now the mutants were stopped and the planet was seemingly peaceful once again.

Suddenly hands of darkness silently rose out of the ground and pulled Diamond down.

"Help...!" but Diamond was gone.

The others heard the plea of help but when they turned around, Diamond was gone.

"Oh no, Diamond." Said Sarah.

Down in a hidden underground lair...

"Wake up, Wake up, WAKE UP!!" yelled someone into Diamond's ear.

"Hey, who the heck…" started Diamond but was cut off by fear.

What she saw was the Emperor of Serpents. The Emperor of Serpents got straight to the point.

"How about you join me, in the dark side, as my apprentice, for your armor?" he said as he reached behind his back and took out the completed and fully repaired Shadow Armor for Diamond.

"It's simple really, to join me you must attack one of your friends and harness evil powers.

"Sorry, but no, even though you have my armor, my friends are more important." Diamond replied.

"Are you sure? Think…" said the Serpent king.

Diamond thought back to her previous days with her friends.

"Hey K.T, want to go to the lake to look for our armor?" asked Diamond.

"We already checked that place ten times!" said Sarah.

"Why not check again?"

"Because it's boring!"

"Fine, I'm going to check and I'm doing to do it alone!" Yelled Diamond.

And she stalked off.

"Still no!" even though Diamond was half considering it.

"Think, with the power of the dark side, you can impress your townsfolk and be always showered with praise whenever you do an impossible job and, also all the people will humiliate your friends because they have less power than you." The Serpent King said.

"I sense superior energy in you, Diamond, too bad you won't realize it until you join me."

"Grrrr, I will find my way out of this lair and when I do, I can find my friends and lead you right to you so they can finish you off!" Diamond yelled as she ran from the room.

"You can run, but you can't stop your destiny..."

Diamond sprinted through the tunnels, stopping at each dead end, and looking for the light at the end of the tunnel, literally!

"Just give in, and then he'll stop chasing you and your friends will respect you." Said a voice in the back of her head.

But Diamond just ignored it, but soon, it became all that she was thinking about. Suddenly, the ground beneath her gave way and found herself tumbling to the earth below. If she didn't do something about it she was going to be smushed. Just as Diamond was twelve feet away from the rough terrain, her body suddenly crackled with the ultimate energy, dark energy. She let it flow through her body and it hurled her up into the air, crashing the ceiling and out onto the surface.

A shadowy figure watched her escape.

"Very good, Diamond, now you've started your journey to the evil." He said. Then he healed the ground and hid his base.

Ch. 19 Lies, anger, and abandoning.

The others saw a black shape burst out of the ground, spreading dust everywhere.

"It's probably the Emperor of Serpents!" yelled Sarah.

"Get him!"

They all ran toward the shape, but when they got there, they got a surprise.

"Diamond, what are you doing, and why are you crackling with the power of the dark side?" asked Max.

Diamond couldn't tell them of her encounter because, that will be traitorous to the Serpent King, but why though? Since her mind had unlocked the power of the darkness an inner Emperor of Serpents had formed and taken control. So she quickly thought up a lie.

"Well, I actually found some of my Armor and was testing it to see if it was safe." She lied.

"Um, then well, SHOW US!!!" yelled K.T

"No way, it is not safe, I just mastered it... duhi, I mean... I can barely control it, I could kill you all if I do activate it." Mumbled Diamond.

Although the others were starting to believe, almost oblivious to Diamonds first words. Max saw treachery through her eyes.

"I'd say that we should just leave Diamond to master her powers and then fetch her." He said sarcastically.

"Oh!! So you're jealous, right!?!" yelled Diamond

"Well, I'm not jealous, but I am concerned about your unity to us!" Max yelled back.

Two tempers were flaring, but that was just the beginning. A big argument followed and K.T and Sarah were dragged into it.

They argued and insulted each other. Diamond's dark side pushed her to even gas as far as insulting Max's family! She then yelled that she regretted even making friends with them.

Finally, as tears of sadness and fury filled Diamond's eyes, and Max's hands were clenched in anger and he was muttering curses under his breath, they swiped their swords out of their belts (Max turned into his Armor) and clashed. The battle seemed as if it lasted for hours but at last, Max made a swipe with his sword at the hilt of Diamonds sword and knocked it put of her grasp. Diamond winced in pain as Max's sword made a cut on her hand.

"Grrrrrrrrrrr…" muttered Diamond.

She raised her hand and fired a bolt of black and navy blue energy and zapped Max.

"Arrrrrrrrrrrrrrrrrrrrggggggggggggggggghhhhhhhhhhhhh!!!!!!!!!! Diamond you traitor!!!!" Yelled Max.

"Oh my gosh, you have betrayed us Diamond, you've joined forces with the Emperor of Serpents!" said K.T.

She just ignored him and continued with her onslaught. Soon, Max was unable to stand and collapsed on the ground. Satisfied, Diamond ran off and abandoned the team.

After she had run a long distance, she punched a hole in the ground and jumped in.

Max was revived and the others were very angry.

"But why though, why did she betray us." Asked Sarah furiously.

"I'd say, as a random guess, she met up with the Serpent king and he promised her great power and glory in return for our death or turning us weak for him to finish us off. I trusted her!" Said K.T answering Sarah's question and shaking with Diamond's betrayal of him.

"We need to find her and take her back, then we can concentrate on the issue of the missing Armor, we need her and your power to activate the Armor, Spirit, Body X fusion." Said Max with great difficulty from pain.

"But wouldn't we be off to a better start if we locate our Armor first?" asked K.T.

"Enough talking, no doubt that our Armor is in hostile places. We've searched for a year and no luck. We can't depend on the Fusion; we need reinforcements." Snapped Sarah as she started running.

Ch 20 Allies

They followed the energy trail that Diamond left behind as she ran. The trail came to be when Diamond was running and some of her power leaked out since she was inexperienced. The trail stopped cold at a specific location.

"That's strange, it just stops ... just like that." Said K.T, puzzled.

"I'll bet you anything that it is a hole, stand back, I'm going to blast it open with water." Said Sarah, pulling out her Elemental blade.

Before you could say "Typhoon Water blast!" Sarah, Max, and K.T were being constricted by a gigantic python, most defiantly a servant of the Serpent king.

"I could, get into my Armor, if my head wasn't swimming from lack of air." Gasped Max.

The team was about to lose their life. They all thought sadly about there parents weeping over their crushed bodies. Also they thought in horror that the Emperor if Serpents could take over the world! It was when hope was just about to be lost when they saw four blurry figures racing towards them and reaching for their weapons. Then all was blank…

"Oh, where are we…"

"Rest…" said a voice.

"Yes, sir… or ma'am…"

Later…

Sarah was awakened with the voice of Max talking.

"Say, who you are and then we can thank you properly." Said Max feverishly.

"Ah, your friend's awake, now we can share, but we must be quiet, for the Emperor of Serpents' spies could be anywhere."

"Yes, go on." Said K.T.

"I am Kai; I have my Earth Armor. This is Sama; she has the Thunder Armor. Corina, my younger sister; she has the Wood Armor. And last, but our most powerful member is Draken; he has the Dragon and Mythical beasts Armor." He finished.

"Sweet!! May we see your Armors? Please, pretty please with whipped cream, chocolate sprinkles, caramel syrup, and a maraschino cherry on top." Pleaded the team.

All of a sudden, there was a flash of light and the four people were in their unique Armor. The kids took a chance to admire them.

Kai's was mostly crafted with silver, with long arm pads. Also the chest, helmet, and thigh armor were the same as K.T's. the rest of the body was lined with hard core granite, but way lighter. Twin spikes, long and powerful, were placed just below the shoulders facing towards the heavens. His weapon was a gigantic hammer.

For a girl, Sama had heavy duty Armor. A large chest plate took up most of the torso. The helmet was lined with thunderbolts. It covered the entire head, with only a face visor. Huge, thick yellow arm pads went up to the elbow, curving up into a triangle, had orbs in them that were containing protons and electrons, waiting to absorb thunder. She had robotic hands. The rest of the Armor looked like the metal plates in the old days, but yellow, much thicker, and had thunderbolts. Her weapon was a lightning bo-staff.

Corina had Sarah's Armor, but was not lined with weapons; instead vines and other vegetation that coils grew up everywhere. Four great big sword ferns grew, two under the shoulder looking at the sky, and two at the waist facing the earth. Also, hemlock wood gloves covered the hands, strong but flexible. Her weapons were a spear made of oak and a whip with thorns.

Finally, Draken's Armor. A ruby and steel helmet of a red dragon's head roaring (a wyvern roaring to be exact). If you looked into the mouth of the red wyvern helmet, you could only see a dark green visor that hid the face. But if you concentrate hard enough you could make out Draken's face. Enormous, feathered, white wings sprouted from the back. An octagonal shield with a griffin on it was on the left arm. He had a sword whose blade was straight, sharp, made of silver, the gold hilt ends were eagle heads with sapphire eyes. His torso and waist armor were crafted out of pure silver, obsidian, and diamond. His legs were the strong hind legs of a fused lion, a wolf, and a T.rex, furry though. Draken's arm armor was just like Sarah's, but the elbow and hands were protected by metal plates.

Max, K.T, and Sarah, all gasped and were stupefied in amazement. These were the champions of the Armor, not just someone who had just used it for good, they had been through intense training!

"We have trailed you, ever since you began your journey for your Armor, well, here it is, all fixed and ready!" announced Sama.

There was a cry and a jump of joy from K.T and Sarah. They held out their hands and,

"KA-ZAM!!!!"

They were all in their full Armor, brimming with power.

"Now, let's find Diamond and take her back!!" the team yelled triumphantly.

Everyone felt a blast of pride, the team had made new, powerful allies who were ready to become their friends and teammates!

The allies held out their hands. "Welcome to the team." They said and shook hands gratefully with the three kids.

Suddenly, Draken yelled, "High five! For the new members of our team!"

Ch 21 Scars of Betrayal

Now we must rush the story all the way to the secret lair of the Emperor of Serpents.

"Ah, yes, Diamond, you have done well, as promised, power is yours."

He shot a beam of green from his Staff of the Ancient Serpent gods and it struck Diamond in the chest. The beam of dark power painfully electrocuted her body. She collapsed on the ground.

"Do not worry, your body needs to adapt to your strength." He whispered and draped the Shadow Armor over her.

Five hours pass…

"I am surging with power, I can disintegrate anyone with just a blast from my hand!" cried Diamond.

As an example, she blew away an entire wall of rock.

"Thanks for my Armor. I'm more tied to the dark power with it." She said gratefully

"Now, since you are my apprentice, you get to control one legion of my snakes. Chose which class. Cobras, mambas, pythons, poisonous and long ones, or mutant animals and snakes." Asked the Serpent king.

"Mutants." Was Diamond's immediate reply.

"Then I guess I'll show you the legion."

He led Diamond into a humungous training room where mutants roamed. Thousands of mutant elephanboonba, buzzaleon, and possessed liontelopes. There were serpents that were totally screwed up. One had five hundred heads, another was as giant as a mountain, some having lethal spikes all over their bodies, some looked normal enough, until they were provoked and became invincible creatures, you never know what they might be.

"This is your new leader! Follow her every command!"

The answer was an ear buster roar.

"Now it is time for your Seal of Loyalty to me."

"What!!! I thought you were just going to give me power, then I can forget you!" yelled Diamond.

The Emperor of Serpents suddenly whipped around and slapped Diamond.

"You didn't think I would let you free, did you?!?! Well no, if you harness the power of the dark side, you must be my apprentice, unless you want to be pushed around by your friends! Now follow me." Snapped the Serpent king.

Reluctantly Diamond followed him into the chamber of Scars.

"I had many apprentices, just some chickened out, some I killed, or some were killed by the good guys." He said, chuckling.

"Grrrrrrrrrrrrrrrrr…" muttered Diamond.

"I see that you are getting angry, good, you'll need all the anger for my test…"

"Huh… What test?" Asked Diamond nervously.

Without warning hundreds of laser bolts zapped her body and weakened her. She screamed cries of fury and her shadow power formed a gigantic half-sphere that grew and blew up all the guns.

"Good, you pass."

Diamond's eyes were glowing red in anger and her skin was turning a bit bluish.

"Now for your scars."

The Emperor of Serpents drew his Serpentall sword and began to draw intricate markings of evil on her flesh all over her body. The markings were like graffiti but they were red and not words. He had to draw them at the right angle or else they are useless. The sharp edges were especially hard. Once a scar was drawn, they would glow blood red. It was a long, long process.

"I liked how you betrayed your friends..." the Serpent King started.

"Former friends." Diamond corrected.

"Yes. Especially that boy that you were in love with. What was his name, K.T.?" The Emperor of Serpents stated.

Diamond just glared at him with revenge in her eyes and growled.

Ch 22 the Search for the Medallion

"Follow me, but be on your guard, the spy snakes can be anywhere." Said Kai, leaving the cave.

"Where are we going?" K.T asked.

"We cannot tell you now, as Kai said, spies can be anywhere." Sama said.

The team walked on, in full Armor. Occasionally, they encountered a mutant, but were annihilated immediately by the power of each of the Champions (the team that rescued K.T, Sarah, and Max).

After a while of walking, Draken flew up and scouted the area, when it was clear, he returned to a clearing.

"Coast is clear; explain to them about the Medallion, Corina."

"Now, we are looking for a great medallion, the jewel on Diamond's head is chipped from the same one. It has superior strength, and it can reverse the effects of Darkness and give bless you with power. But it still remains hidden, after one year of looking for it."

"How old are you people?" Asked Sarah, totally off topic.

"Well, I'm twelve, Sama is thirteen, Sis is the youngest, at eleven, and Draken is fourteen." Said Kai.

"Now let's get back to the topic, do you have any clues to where the medallion is?" asked Max.

"We do, but the letters are in an ancient beast tongue, we can only guess on the pictures, and most of the script was lost during a raid from great pythons." Said Draken, "and I can't read them."

"Let us take a look at it and maybe we'll find something new." Said Max.

Inside the Plateau of Golems, in a secret cave…

"Here are the remaining scripts…"

"So there you have it, the carvings." Said Corina.

"The medallion thingy looks like what the medallion is." Said Sarah, "Perhaps we ought to call it the Entwined Dragons."

"Okay, now for the other two,"

"The one with the landscape, I think is the location, the stone dragon head is probably where the Entwined Dragons is placed. And I don't know about the fourth one." Said Max.

"Wait; hold on a minute, I can read some of it …" said K.T.

"where mountains float and rocks spin, orichalckos by sliver, gold by iron, the Entwined Dragons were made.

"Search the stones of the Valley of … I couldn't understand that part…

"remove… this word is confusing… *gray waterfall…*

"Play on the enchanted obsidian serpent flute… *enter the portal of weirdness,* Huh?? Okay… *there you will find the Entwined Dragons."*

"Wow, how did you learn that?" asked Draken, astonished.

"Oh, just from the History Geeks Magazines I order every month." Said K.T.

"So, I think we have to go to the birthing place of the Entwined Dragons." Said Sama.

"But where is that?" asked Corina.

"Perhaps I know, Said Draken, I found my Armor in that place, remember team. It was when we were attacked by the Emperor of Serpents and his Eagle demons. I don't know how he got in but the place is the Valley of Beginnings."

The Champions had a moment where they all looked dreamy and smiled. The moment was so clear in their heads.

"Then, uh, where is it?" asked Sarah.

"It is in a place where only people with pure souls and hearts can go, or in other words, people who have no evil or greed or anything that was out of the Pandora's Box except hope." Said Kai.

"What would happen if evil tried to enter?" Max asked.

"Mostly a shield would come up and they would not be able to penetrate. But if they are the purest evil, the shield would electrify them into ashes." said Corina.

"Maybe we should split up, Kai you come with us to take Diamond back; we need your elemental power." Said K.T.

"Done." Everyone said.

After a mile of walking, Corina cocked her head to one side and held a finger to cup her ear as to enhance her hearing.

"Hear that?" she asked.

"Yeah, sounds like…"

"Get down!" yelled Draken.

A huge cobra ripped through the clearing and went

"Hissssssssssssssssssssssssssssssssssssssss!!!"

Sama burst into her Armor and launched a bolt of electrical power from her lightning bo-staff. Hit!!

The current flowed through the python and shocked it black.

"Tell us what you are doing, and no one gets hurt." Said Corina.

"I was supposed to stalk you, and attack you when it was time." It replied in its own tongue, Draken translated.

"How did you know that we were here?" asked Corina.

"My master told me. Speak of the devil, here he comes." The python said.

The Emperor of Serpents crashed through the trees and with him came Diamond.

The change in her was so evident that the Champions almost fainted in shock.

Her skin was almost gray, and her eyes were a glowing blood red. Also, when Draken switched to a vision that can see evil scars, the scars were all over her body, except on her right hand. Diamond outstretched her hands and shot three Shadow Spheres. They encased the three heroes and started to suffocate them. The Emperor of Serpents gave her a nod of approval.

"Good, good, now, what do you want to do with them, my apprentice?" He asked.

"Let's force them to guide us to the Valley of Beginnings." Replied Diamond, looking up at the Emperors ugly face with a hint of coldness in her voice.

"Never! We'd rather die than show you the sacred and holy place!!" yelled Corina.

"Humph, fine, die here, I will rely on my hyper-accurate memory to locate it." The Serpent King said.

And he started to walk north, the exact opposite of the direction the Valley was!!!

"SUCKER!!" yelled Sama as he walked away, not hearing the insult.

"Now, how are we going to get out of here, I feel faint…"

Those were Corina's last words before falling unconscious.

"Hang on."

Suddenly, Draken's shadow cage was burnt into a crisp by a phoenix that swooped out of the blue sky. Its flame was as scorching as the Sun's core itself!!! So, as you know already, the inferno melted all of the spheres and the phoenix perched itself on Draken's shoulder. He tickled it under the chin, dismissed it, and it disappeared.

"Wow, how could you summon up a phoenix?!?" asked Sama.

"I have the Dragon and Mythical beasts Armor, what do you expect?" replied Draken.

"Doh! My short term memory loss disease is acting up again." Said Sama, whapping her head.

"Anyway, the Emperor of Serpents is stalled for a few hours; perhaps we can make it to the Valley before he can."

"Psyche!" someone yelled.

And snakes came flying out of nowhere and wrapped themselves around the team…

Ch 23, The Prophesy

The rest of the group had no idea that the others were in trouble, but were tracking down the remains of the wisps of energy that Diamond left behind and followed them. After a few minutes Kai held his arm out to signal "Stop".

"This is the hollow ground." He said.

"How do you know?"

"I sense it through my Armor."

"I'm going to blast it open with water." Said Sarah, pulling out her Elemental blade, again.

"No! There may be a booby trap or something." Cautioned Max.

"Nah, it couldn't be, I mean, the Emperor of Serpents is arrogant, and he thinks that nobody can find it." Kai replied.

Sarah blew it open with a precise shot of water and they braced themselves… nothing happened.

"Ha!! See, what did we tell you! No trap!"

They descended into the lair.

The lair was pitch black, so Max pulled out his Elemental blade, transformed the sword into flames and it lit up the whole cavern.

"Wow, look at all the strange carvings here."

"They are probably timelines, like the ones that the primitive humans did." Said K.T.

"Look at one of them." Said Max

It was one that revealed the secrets of the Serpent King's power. The pictures were (in order): the Serpent King fighting with the original Heroes of the New World, absorbing their power, learning how to purify his soul for as long as he wanted, and actually creating the Entwined Dragons!!! By grabbing a Darkness Dragon and a Light Dragon and entwining them.

"Holy cow! The Entwined Dragons is evil; we must meet up with the others and destroy the medallion." Exclaimed Kai.

"But how? Won't destroying it ruin the balance of Nature?" asked K.T.

The team looked at him as if he had nine heads and feet.

"Haven't you figured it out? The Dragons are Yin and Yang!"

"So… the creator of the whole universe is… the Emperor of Serpents?!" exclaimed Max.

"Yes."

"Now I feel dirty, unpurified, because now I know that this Armor I'm wearing is a part of the Serpent King." Said Kai.

"No wonder we couldn't destroy the Emperor with the Fusion, because the Armors were a bit of him." Sarah said sadly.

"Evil cannot defeat evil, only good can do that." Said K.T.

"But how can we destroy him if we cannot rely on our Armors?" Max asked.

"Remember these…" said K.T, pulling out his Elemental blade.

"Sure!"

"But hold on, didn't the Serpent king tell us that he came here only some years ago? If he did, how could he make the Universe?" asked Sarah.

The team pondered over that for a bit.

"He's lying." Concluded Max.

"But why would he want to blow up his own planet?" asked Sarah, again.

"He wants to control the Universe, remember?" replied Max, again.

They started to walk further into the Chamber when Kai's sharp eyes spotted something covered by dust and some wood on the Wall.

"Wait, what is this?" said Kai.

Kai brushed away the dust covering, pulled down the wood and found that portion of the wall was deeper than the rest of the Wall. Suddenly a king cobra sprang out, fangs bared. Kai just snatched it out of the air and slammed it into the wall, a killing blow. The team leaned in closer to get a better look at what was inside the gap.

"What the hey…"

The team looked at the carving. It was (In order) Diamond being the Emperor of Serpents' apprentice, then betraying her friends, the friends kidnap her back, purify her, the whole team except Diamond transfer their powers, spirit, and body into her Elemental blade, her blade transforms into an awesome sword, and her destroying the Serpent King.

"No wonder this was guarded. The Serpent King doesn't want to see this nor does he want anyone else to witness this!" exclaimed Sarah.

"Wow, we must tell the others about this and get Diamond back!" yelled Kai, already racing to the hole.

Meanwhile, we are rushing back to the rest of the Champions…

The slithery snakes' scaly and smooth bodies wrapped around them quite quickly. Very soon, they were on the ground like sacks of potatoes. The Serpent King came over and kicked Sama on the cheek with his fleshy foot and said,

"You are very impolite to the ruler of this world. Calling me a sucker, yeesh, that is harsh on me. By the way, I have good ears so I heard the insult. Let me tell you something. I created the universe, so I'm the rightful ruler."

The Champions' eyes widened in shock. They tried to yell out but the snakes had bound themselves also around their mouth.

"Pledge your alliance to me, and I'll spare your life." Said the Serpent King.

"Never!" yelled the Champions.

Diamond watched on as the Emperor taunted them and questioned Sama. But he was soon filled with frustration because of her short term memory loss. She had depression in her heart and mind. She used to be one of them, one of the light, but now, she had turned her back on them and the light.

Suddenly, she felt a searing pain in her head as she was thinking.

"Oh-ho, so that's the side affect of these scars, whenever I think of my deeds of the past... when I was in the side of light... I get a pain so I can forget about them completely." Diamond said in her head.

All of a sudden, she had a brainwave!

"This is revenge for making me have headaches whenever I think of my friends, even if I'm on the dark side."

She was the general of the mutants, and those snakes are within her power because they are mutants. She snapped her fingers, and the serpents swelled to an enormous size. Since there were so many snakes, they lost grip of the Champions. All of a sudden, a blur of black and yellow swished by and snatched up the Champions.

"What are you doing!?" yelled the Emperor of Serpents furiously.

"I...I thought that if the snakes grew bigger, they would have more of a chance of crushing the Armor Wielders." Replied Diamond.

Unexpectedly, an explosion ripped through the trees and the Serpent King was caught in a raging cyclone of fire, rock, and electricity. Then, out of the sky, a jet of water collided with the cyclone and produced a fog. During the confusion, Diamond heard the beating of wings, the scratch, scratch and soft thumps of talons and lion paws on dirt, extremely familiar voices. Strong hands grabbed her and took her away up into the sky on a griffin. She tried to struggle but the grip was too much like granite, almost like real granite. She gave herself up as dead when she blacked out from too much pain of being close to someone so pure in light.

Ch 24, The cure

When she was back in conscious, her mind was vague and couldn't see clearly, but could hear out talking.

"Good thing that the alarm sounded just before the Emperor started carving her right hand. He couldn't risk a mistake so he postponed it until later."

"Yeah."

"So you think that the Serpent King's lair is the ancient Chamber of Records and Prophecy?"

"Yes, we saw the fabled legend of the destruction of the Emperor…"

That was enough to rouse Diamond. She jumped from her bed and raised her hand, emitting a signal for all mutants to gather at that spot.

She listened for the thundering noise as she confronted her former friends. Her powers were at their peak and she let loose her fury at them.

"So you're awake, long time no see, Diamond." Said K.T, grinning, even though Diamond was yelling herself hoarse.

All their exploits came rushing into Diamond's head as soon as she heard the cool voice of K.T. and she almost had tears of joy of seeing their good deeds again. But she shoved those thoughts to the back of her brain and said nothing.

"You too ashamed to even say a hello?" asked Corina.

"Awwww, is the little evil girl afraid that we might destroy your master? Don't worry, we will destroy him. All prophecies do come true" Draken said, mockingly.

That was enough goading to get Diamond irritated. Her hand automatically rose and acid blasted. The team dodged it with ease. Then Diamond tried blowing up the whole base by creating a Shadow Explosion. But that failed because of Draken unleashing a Lion of light. It was a lion the size of a small elephant brimming with light so it repelled the explosion. Really frustrated, she launched herself at them, fists clenched and brimming with even mightier Shadow Power. But that was just what the Champions wanted her to do. As she charged, they side-stepped and tripped her, then fastened her with an enchanted chain. Nothing could break it, and I mean NOTHING!!!

Diamond was struggling and yelling curses and insults and threats so Max took a cloth and gagged her.

"So, Corina, you're our natural healer, know any cures for these scars?" Draken asked once everything was quiet.

Corina thought for a moment.

"Well, there is one and only cure, take one drop of her blood, add one drop of ours, mix it, and let her drink it, then she must be exposed to a crescent moon, and finally, drop a pint of pure light into the gem on her head." she replied.

"So, we don't wrench out the gem?" asked Draken.

"Yes."

Diamond's eyes widened with a nauseous feeling in her stomach as they slit a slight cut in her skin, let a drop of blood fall into a vial, and watch them sacrifice a drop of their blood to the vial. Max took the vial, took off her gag and forced the concoction into her mouth. She drank it.

Diamond could feel pain surge through her veins as all her dark blood was being cleansed. She writhed and struggled and closed her eyes to make the pain stop. After a few moments of torture the light faded, along with the scars.

"Wahoo!" the team yelled.

"Not so fast, we need to get rid of the Dark spirit inside her." Said K.T.

"It's nearly the midnight, and today is a crescent moon." Said Sarah, checking her watch.

So they dragged Diamond outside and made her look into the moon. It was bright. Without warning, her shadow soul erupted from her chest and bellowed in agony. Some minutes later, when the dark spirit was about to be vanquished, a cloud covered the moon.

The weakened shadow soul slithered back into Diamond's body.

"Oh no! Her shadow soul still lives!" wailed Draken.

"Don't worry; the truly evil part of the soul has been banished; only the *energy*, the attacks remain." Said Corina calmly.

"Now here comes the hard part, where do we find a pint of pure light?" Max asked.

They talked and talked and talked, but no one could find a solution.

"I think we should leave it at this step, the true shadow soul has been destroyed." Said Max.

"Yeah, and the dark powers could be valuable on our quests." Said K.T happily.

"Ahh, the mutants, we forgot about them." Exclaimed Draken.

The mutants stood no match for the Champions. They cut them down in an instant.

So that was that. The rest of the month was used to train for a final and all out battle between good and evil. They sent a messenger to report that the victor of a war will have Planet Mythical Peace. (The world that they were on, if you forgotten). Diamond apologized to her friends for turning to the dark side and thanked her friends for getting her back.

"It was so weird using dark powers and seeing so many scars on your body." Diamond said.

Her most effective power is letting her dark side take over. Then she became a rampaging warrior. It was only used as a last resort. But when she was in Dark mode, she had blood red eyes, her scars were back and her weapons and fighting style were totally different. She had a scythe that can slice through anything and a Dark Chain to back up the scythe. Also her martial arts were not just cool kicks and punches, they were lighting-quick, bone-breaking blows.

The rest of the month later…

Ch 25, War

There was no peace. The Emperor of Serpents kept on sending legions of snakes and mutants to assassinate the team. They could not settle down. So to end these ongoing assaults of them, the Champions declared war on the Emperor.

"OK, so here's the plan. Corina, Draken, Kai and I will take on the Serpent King's legions; the rest of you will wait in ambush after we are done. If the Emperor of Serpents makes a move, tries anything to harm us while we are fighting, attack!" said Max.

"Yeah, but what if he tries to attack you first off, then what?" asked Sarah.

"Then we will have a full force assault."

"What about me?" asked Diamond.

"You unleash your Dark powers. But be careful not to wipe us out with the creatures that you are fighting." Said Kai, grinning.

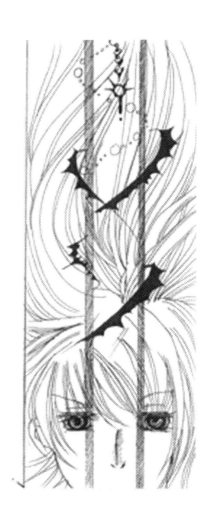

"But, for sure he will bring his invincible mutant snakes." Said Diamond and told them about those special kind of serpents.

"Then we will just fight them until their invincibility wears off." Said Kai.

"A risky plan indeed, but it is a risk we will have to take. Diamond, you can control when you want to suck your shadow soul back into your body, right?" asked K.T.

"Yeah."

"Good, so when all the Serpent King's army has been depleted, we all draw ourselves into Diamond's blade and then she'll destroy the Emperor of Serpents once and for all." Replied K.T.

At the location were the Nightmare Mountains used to be…

The ruins of the Nightmare Mountains were overcome by lush vegetation and undergrowth. People could hardly relate the Mountains of Shadow and Fire to the place that it is now."

"So, everyone ready?" asked Draken.

They all nodded and took their positions. But what they forgot to discuss was Sama's short term memory loss, and the moment she took her position she instantly forgot what she was supposed to do.

"What are we doing again?" she asked the others.

"Ahhh, no! Okay, so we are waiting in ambush for…" started Sarah.

"Shhhhhhhhh!" whispered K.T. "They're here."

It was true; the Emperor of Serpent's mutant and serpent army had arrived.

Max and the others had started fighting. Sama took that as a signal and rushed into the fray, armor activated.

"Oh-no! The plan is ruined!" yelled K.T.

Even with the ruined plan, the group was making good progress; already a quarter of the army was demolished. Max with his swords and wolves. Sama with her lightning Bo-staff. Corina with her spear and whip. Kai with his Earth Hammer. And Draken with the aid of dragons and Mythical beasts and himself riding Pegasus and slashing off heads with his sword. The Serpent King saw where Sama came from and guessed that they were planning an ambush.

"So be it." The Emperor thought in his mind.

And with that he released a torrent of sharp and poisonous energy darts from his hand at the hiding place. K.T had to grab everyone and run smack into the battlefront.

So it was an all out war. The Champions were doing wonders, but it was Diamond who was the main soldier. She had with her own power, killed half of the legions with good speed. It was when the Serpent King sensed that they were getting exhausted he let loose the invincibility serpents to finally conquer good once and for all.

Max saw them coming, he alerted everyone to retreat, but asked Diamond to stay and try to tire them. The snakes were gigantic! Their poison could melt a hole in the ground all the way down to the core of this planet.

Diamond fought like she never fought before. Before her attacks were short. Now she is reaching the speed of light and the strength of eighty million elephants! But the mutant snakes were persistent. Shields were erected every time she made an attack. By now, her shadow soul was nearly consumed of its power.

Suddenly, K.T realized something.

"Diamond, stop!" He yelled.

"K.T? Are you crazy?" yelled Kai.

"No, we can use the fusion since we are fighting servants of the Serpent King, not the Serpent King himself!" K.T said, full of excitement.

"Right!" said the others.

Max, Sarah, Diamond, and K.T linked hands and nodded.

"Armor, Spirit, Body X Fusion!" They all cried and suddenly there was an explosion of light. The outline of four figures slowly merged into one. When the light subsided, the team was united, just like one year ago.

"Let's go!"

The Fusion got all the explosives in one hand and threw them. The detonation ripped through the valley and stunned the invincible snakes. Next, it combined the powers of Diamond's, K.T's and Max's Armor to create Shadow Spheres that trapped the Serpents. What more, inside the Spheres it was -100 degrees Celsius and thanks to K.T's speed Armor, the serpents were bouncing speedily around in the sphere, hitting the hard walls of shadow. Finally, the Fusion absorbed back the spheres and yelled:

"Ultimate Dragon Punch of the Ancient Power Armors!!!"

The punch totally obliterated the mutants. And who said that they were invincible. Law, everything in the whole wide world has a weakness.

Now for the Emperor of Serpents. The Fusion "Defused" and became the team again.

Ch 26, the final battle

"Okay, concentrate all your energy into Diamond's Elemental blade." Said Sama seeing that Diamond had drawn her blade out of her belt.

Everyone focused every fiber of his or her power into the sword. When Draken opened his eyes again, he felt normal.

"I don't think it worked." He said.

"Guess again."

He looked around and saw the others were confined as swirling colour.

"So this is what the inside of an Elemental blade looks like, cool"

Diamond and the Emperor of Serpents hacked, slashed, and blocked with their swords. But none of them was ever showing tiredness. Neither of them could do damage because they were equal in strength and skill. The Serpent King backed Diamond against a tree and tried to "Scissor Cut" her in half. (The Scissor cut is when you have two swords and you cross-slash them at the same time. In the Emperor of Serpents' case, his second blade was his scythe on his right hand.)

But Diamond, using the power of K.T's Armor was too nimble to be sliced and the Emperor of Serpents chopped the tree in half. However, the Serpent King was expecting something like a dodge and quickly stooped and knocked Diamond off balance with his leg. She jumped back to her feet and grabbed her sword. They hopped onto a ledge and forced each other back. The Serpent King twirled his blade round and round until he lashed forward and disarmed Diamond. She summoned her Armor powers to grab back her sword but it was too late, the Emperor of Serpents had kicked her over her side of the ledge and she fell. The impact was painful when she hit and it almost knocked her unconscious. The Serpent King followed her. Diamond suddenly rolled under his legs and seized them, hauling him down smack on the hard dirt. Angrily he sprung back on his feet, saw that she had retrieved her blade, and hurled his sword furiously at Diamond. She had nowhere to move to avoid being hit. Her only option was to parry, and she did. With such force that the strength of Kai's Earth Armor donated to Diamond, her blade knocked the sword away and actually shattered it! The sight of the ruined sword gave her new integrity, endurance, and strength. Diamond rushed at the Emperor, jumped, and cut off his right hand so he didn't have a weapon, and with a lightning quick turn she severed his body in half. Then it was the blade that did this; it delivered rapid slashes to his torso. After that the Serpent King collapsed.

"Ha! That's done! Evil is gone forever!" Diamond yelled.

"Think again."

The Serpent King was up, but he was growing, and growing, and growing. Soon he was as tall was a skyscraper. Also, he looked different. His head was the same, but his legs and feet were the ones of a dragon. Also, he had dragon wings. His left arm was a giant bear's. His right arm was human, but was lined with spikes. His voice was deep, dark, and evil.

"Can you eliminate me, now?!!!" he said full of evil.

"Yes, somehow." Whispered Diamond.

"Ah, so confident, now so fearful, don't fret, all your troubles will be over, in the afterlife!" he bellowed and threw a punch with his right hand. Diamond leaped out of the way, but not before the one of the spikes bashed off a part of the hilt. The magical energies of the Elemental blade leaked out, including the team.

Diamond tried to use what was left of the sword to cut through the feet, but now, without any magical energy, it was just a plain sword and didn't even penetrate. The Emperor of Serpents raised a foot and brought it down on Diamond.

"No!" yelled the others.

Diamond was okay, but she had just barely escaped death by creating a shadow sphere around herself and rolling to safety with her team.

"Got any plans?"

"Yes!" said Corina.

"What?"

"K.T, Sarah, Max, and Diamond, hand me your swords please."

They handed them to Corina who merged them into one.

"There, all done, now you have a Super Elemental Blade. And here, Draken's sword for a spare."

"Hey!"

"Don't worry, you'll get it back."

"Fine. But what if she breaks it?"

"Well, we'll forge you a new one." She replied.

"I always knew you were a brilliant and clever girl, sis" said Kai.

"Thank you, big bro." Corina replied.

"Thanks guys." Diamond said to her friends as they dove inside the Super Elemental Blade.

While they were talking, the Emperor of Serpents was bleaching out poison gas to wither the trees and bring destruction.

"Done yet?!" the Emperor of Serpents was impatient.

"Okay, let's go!!"

Diamond's hyper-speed allowed her to race up the Serpent King's feet and sliced them up. As soon as the feet were gone, a tornado took up the legs. His right arm burst into roaring flames, left arm into water, and torso into hard core granite. Further more, he grew a tail made of diamond.

"I absorb anything, even the power of the Elements in your blade."

"Oh boy, how can I defeat something that can absorb my attacks... wait, I know, I'll use that to my advantage..." Diamond thought.

She activated the fire element in her sword and the blade turned into blazing fire. She ran into the tornado.

Before she could enter, the Serpent King rammed his left hand into the twister and it became a waterspout.

"Heh."

Diamond knew that it was almost suicidal to go into that, but she had no choice. Holding her breath, she jumped in.

The raging water almost extinguished the blade, but Diamond held her head and made a slice to the wall of moisture.

When the first slice of the fire blade was executed, the Emperor of Serpents bellowed with triumph as he transformed into a being of fire.

Diamond's skin burned. She closed her eyes and used K.T's speed to jump out.

Without hesitation, she let loose a tsunami. As fire and water collided, the Serpent King became a creature of steam. He could have become a creature of water but since the attack was so sudden his absorbing molecules couldn't keep up.

"NOOOOO!!!" he yelled.

Before the Emperor of Serpents could rise to the clouds, Diamond slammed the point of the sword into the ground and a fissure opened up underneath the Serpent King.

"Ahhh!" he screamed as he fell down into the chasm. Diamond made the chasm close.

"Oh, great." Diamond muttered.

A colossal stone hand erupted from the ground to grasp Diamond. During that process, the sword's blade was shattered.

Before most of the magic spilled out, she grabbed Draken's sword and merged the damaged sword with it.

"Wood!!!" she yelled and drove the blade into the hand. Vines and undergrowth started winding down the hand and constricting it. The hand lost its grip on Diamond because of shock, so she jumped down and landed lightly before a green glow came over the hand. The Serpent King was now a beast of vines, roots, and plants.

"Yes, my perfect chance!" shouted Diamond triumphantly as she unleashed a powerful fire blast.

When the blast made contact, the Emperor of Serpents exploded into flames.

"Argh, the fire weakens me, ah the pain of fire!" he shrieked.

All of a sudden, the fire dispersed. He was back in his original, big form.(the one with the dragon wings and stuff like that)

"Ouch, that weakened me..." the Serpent King's mouth widened. "No, don't get any ideas..."

Diamond grinned.

"Ready guys?" she asked the sword.

And the sword sent a reply to her mind.

"Ready as always!"

"Good." Diamond replied.

She glowed as she bristled with the energies of the Super Elemental Blade.

"Dragon and Mythical beasts Armor!" she yelled.

And a carving of a dragon encircled the handle and at the ends of the hilt two lion heads were in.

"Earth Armor!"

And the blade became a kind of crystal that is one hundred times harder than diamond and still very light.

"Thunder Armor!"

And electricity was sparking around the granite blade.

"Wood Armor!"

Vines grew on the hilt and a bit of the handle and blade.

"Speed Armor!"

The colour of the sword handle and hilt became black with thunderbolts.

"Weapon Armor!"

Two gun barrels that fired lasers sprouted on the hilt of the sword.

"Werewolf and Ice Armor!"

An arctic blue aura glowed around the whole sword and a small gold wolf head appeared just above the hilt.

"And Shadow Armor!"

"What? Will the Shadow Armor even work?!" the Emperor of Serpents asked.

"Yes!"

With that a black aura lined the outside of the blue aura.

Now Diamond had the Omega Sword.

"This is for trying to convert me to the Dark side, mutating innocent animals, and trying to kill my friends." She yelled and charged.

At that moment, her body surged with joy, extreme happiness, determination, and a tinge of sadness because evil was going to be annihilated! But the tinge of sadness was that there will be no more fun because there will be no more evil butt-kicking.

Diamond rocketed in the air when she made a powerful jump. When the Serpent King spewed poison gas, acid, and chain lightning, Diamond just cut through it. Still she took some damage. She reached the Emperor of Serpent's chest, made a mighty slash with the blade, jumped in, shot and sliced everything with the laser guns and blade, damaging his internal organs, and chopped her way out. On her leap out, Diamond spun so rapidly that she rose and slashed the Serpent King's head off.

When she returned to the ground, the Emperor of Serpents picked up his decapitated skull and said,

"You are strong... but more evil is on the way... more powerful than me... still, you are the rightful winner...I lose."

Those were his last words before he exploded.

Diamond set free everyone and returned Draken's sword

"The prophecy is fulfilled, you destroyed the Serpent King!" Said Max.

"You handled that blade well! We're so proud of you!" said Sarah.

"Well, you guys should take some credit as well, since you were the ones who gave me all the power and energy." Replied Diamond.

"I guess." Said Sama.

"Wait, I'm going to check to see if any particles of the Emperor of Serpents remain…"

Diamonds placed her hand on the ground and spread a collector shadow. Give it something to collect and it will get it. The shadow returned with nothing.

"Wahoo! High Five everybody." Yelled K.T.

Everyone jumped up and slapped each others hand.

"Let's have a celebration!" everybody yelled

"Let's have hot dogs!" Max yelled out."

Everyone looked at him.

"Well it is a good place to start!" said Draken.

They all laughed.

In the city…

"There, a hot dog stand!" pointed Kai.

"Four original, two beef, and two veggie dogs please." Said Sama.

"Right away."

The hot dog seller showed her face.

"Mrs. Dinklebutt?!" the children yelled.

"You?!" Mrs. Dinklebutt yelled.

"What are you doing here?" K.T asked.

"I got fired."

The team burst out laughing.

"Anyway, try the hot dogs, they're delicious. That is why my stand is called Fantastic Hot Dogs." She said.

"Lame." Commented Max.

They took the first bite.

"This is terrific."

"Absolutely fabulous."

"Scrumptious."

The kids made their peace with Mrs. Dinklebutt, paid, and left for home to be with their parents again.

That night, a huge party was held in Max's house, being it the biggest house of all the kids. Everyone danced, ate, played all the way until morning.

The daily lives were resumed. The damage to Diamond was that she got asthma, a few blisters on the face, and the occasional headaches. Also it seems as if, when the Emperor of Serpents was destroyed, all the mutants and all the snakes under his rule disintegrated into dust.

The planet was peaceful and rid of evil once more… for now.

REMEMBER, KIDS CAN BE HEROES TOO.
SO DON'T THINK WE KIDS ARE HELPLESS, WE CAN HELP YOU ADULTS!!!

 To all of you that might have been offended by this book, my most sincere apologies to you.

 "That Kid was born in 1995.

 "I started my writing career at age 7, with my own version of really horrible Captain Underpants comic books. Soon it became a hobby. In the spring break of grade four I was bored, so my mother suggested me to write a short novel to pass the time. After two months, I finished it (although it was screwy and just plain bad), with confidence to continue with more and more novels. Over time, I had finished another two novels. I had a lot of help from many friends and others. Other hobbies I enjoy are eating, reading, daydreaming and gaming systems. I live with my family, in Vancouver B.C."

 Also, I made up the pen name, "That Kid" because my school principal for four years didn't know my name. I even sent an e-mail to him about something and I didn't get a reply. I waited for a couple of weeks before I asked and he had a blank expression and suddenly the principal remembered.

 "Oh, you're that kid who sent me the e-mail!"

 That's were the pen name "That Kid" came from.

PART ONE
An attempt to return home is transformed into an epic quest to save a planet.

Four kids board a subway that takes them to another planet. What starts as a journey to the Hell Mountains and to a pathway back home becomes a quest to save a planet from destruction. Along the way, the kids find their own unique armor and master the special abilities. After many battles, they learn who is behind all the evil and have to battle the enemy who is planning to destroy the peaceful planet.

After the battle, it's a race against time to evacuate Earth from the exploding Sun.

PART TWO
The enemy is reborn and he has kidnapped a friend from the kids.

The kids are currently searching or their destroyed armor, but suddenly one of their friends has transferred to the dark side. They will encounter many difficulties and meet new allies. But the real challenge is, will they be able to fight one of their own friends and turn her back into the light? And will their combined power be enough to defeat their most dangerous foe that can absorb anything that you attack him with?

Don't miss the coming book,
"The New World.
Quest for the Beasts."

Printed in the United States
64659LVS00001B/37-72

9 781425 960520